NIVEN GOVINDEN

*All the
Days and
Nights*

The Friday Project
An imprint of HarperCollins*Publishers*
1 London Bridge Street
SE1 9GF

www.harpercollins.co.uk

First published by The Friday Project in 2014
This paperback edition first published 2015

978-0-00-811343-8

Typeset in Janson Text by Palimpsest Book Production Ltd, Falkirk, Stirlingshire

Printed and bound in Great Britain by Clays Ltd, St Ives plc

MIX
Paper from
responsible sources
FSC
www.fsc.org   FSC® C007454

FSC™ is a non-profit international organisation established to promote
the responsible management of the world's forests. Products carrying the
FSC label are independently certified to assure consumers that they come
from forests that are managed to meet the social, economic and
ecological needs of present and future generations,
and other controlled sources.

Find out more about HarperCollins and the environment at
www.harpercollins.co.uk/green

I leave you my portrait so that you will have my presence all the days and nights that I am away from you.
Frida Kahlo

I do not trouble my spirit to vindicate itself or be understood.
Walt Whitman

WHERE WERE YOU when the sky collapsed; rain falling in pinched sheets, but constant, and the mist descending as if gravity was its master, until it settled on the front step and the path? Was the sky in collusion? Had you conspired with the elements to stay hidden from me; not satisfied with withholding so much of yourself, now your physical body had to be hidden too? Your intentions have brought the mist. You have unsettled nature. The swallows nesting above the window fret over what is to come. They scratch the roofing felt with urgency and speak their fear with a caw that rises from the pull of their guts. How instinctive their talk is, how deeply felt. The cassette spool from the answering machine in the hall hums and burrs more audibly than before, making me think of a hornets' nest under the bed; each creature whirled into a fury and ready to break out. Everything is angry. But what signal is ours? What cry or call will reach you, muffled by cloud, lost in the mist? The dank has whitewashed the landscape, reducing you to a wisp, a dot in the meadow. Is this where I have driven you: into the chill of first light, to be soaked to the skin, slipping on the edge of the path as gravel gives way to mud as you walk toward town and the store that is not yet open, but the rail station that is, and the incoming train that will take you away from me, if you have decided that this is the day? There will be nothing in your pockets bar the silver-edged

1

comb that belonged to your father and your frayed notebook, wedged in the back and struggling to be held. There will be no metallic clink as you walk, keys left behind and no money to speak of, but if you have decided, woken from the bed on the other side of this wall and filled with the determination you've previously threatened, you will find a way to be on that train, through charm, or theft, or an attempt at forced entry. Reviving the same hobo spirit that brought you here. If this is the day.

But it isn't, is it? I know you too well to be crippled by surprise. You forget how I hear your footsteps as you creep down the stairs. Even in your stealth I can read you; the difference between the tiptoe to the doorway of the outbuilding where you punch your frustrations into the hay bales stored there; the steps that lead to the liquor cupboard in the middle of the night, when you believe that I am asleep, and not numbed enough to follow. A man, seventy years old, with the furtive steps of a teenager. Then those that take you to the bottom of the path, where you stand in your shirt and jeans, the same as when you arrived, hesitating at the gate before turning back. Innumerable times I've seen you at the gate, a shadow filling the cleft in your chin, the rising motion as your face twists southward to take in the house, deciding whether you have had enough of it. When you no longer lift your head, when there is no pause, fingers not drumming on the latch, where the echo of flesh pounding metal falls flat against the window and culls the ringing in my ears, I'll know. Until then, we'll carry on as before, in our spurts of comfort and unease. You will continue to sit and I will continue to paint you, because that, John, is why you are here.

Vishni burns the coffee. She is distracted by the thickness of the rain and the absence of you. Usually she would wake to find the fire in the kitchen lit, the stove light on, possibly some voices in heated argument on the radio; whether Carter can hold his own against Reagan; new anger for a new decade; one of the few things from the outside world that interests you. She expects these things and today they are not there, disturbing her in a way she had not anticipated. She stands in the darkness of a barely broken morning for several minutes, wondering if there was a note mentioning a business trip she had forgotten, or whether she had paid scant attention to the clock before leaving her room. She wrings the excess bathwater that has soaked her plaited hair into the sink before re-coiling it into a bun, all the time, thinking. An epoch of wondering passes until I hear the rip of the light cord as the rise and fall is pulled. You never sleep late, nor leave the house without some kind of welcome for her. She is undecided whether to march or creep up the stairs and so manages a little of both. The door of your bedroom is opened in the same confused manner and then closed again within seconds, the final crack of the handle pulled hard against the door frame and ringing through the hall. This is Vishni all over: covert but ultimately clumsy. Bureau drawers not entirely closed and overdue bills stuffed roughly back into envelopes are typical of her handiwork. There is nothing to see there: the bed will be made, the curtains drawn. If I had the voice I could save her the futility. At our ages, we think of economy in all things. She is breathless with exertion, her heavy lungs punishing her for this impulsiveness. As she stands outside my room, more hesitant than before, her wheezy rasp seeps through the gap under the door. She knows it is unlikely that you will be here but wishes to be thorough. The door handle rattles with her uncertainty, to wake me with a knock or ease the door open to spy on someone who despises being watched, who has made a career of being invisible.

– What is it?

– I was looking for John, Anna.

– I sent him to the store. We ran out of one of the oils last night. Had to finish early because of it.

Lightness appears in Vishni's voice – relief – betraying that she too shared the same thoughts.

– Let me get the fire going. I'll have breakfast ready for when he returns.

She is only here for you; enjoys your company and pandering to your needs. Coffee is served how you like it, breakfast and other meals to your whims. It's why we often eat like children: franks and beans, macaroni with everything. On those mornings when your presence at the table is shortened because of the need for firewood or household repair, the tone is quite different. The radio is mostly switched off. She will not sit and watch me eat. No teasing passes between us. The offer of second helpings when the plate is clean is only made the once, both of us understanding that mothering cannot be applied here. We are left as two women thinking about their respective work, aware of the other's presence, but still in our separate spheres.

When you first moved here, I warned you of my need for silence and space. You warned me of your need to eat

4

something that was not raw or burnt. Vishni has been here almost as long as you, following barely a month after your arrival. See how quickly I acted for you back then! Your every intelligent suggestion was my command. I wonder if you even remember the nights I spent away from my work to call people I knew in the town asking for recommendations; people who were alarmed at hearing my voice at the end of the receiver, having been aware of my long-standing reticence toward the telephone, and believing that I would only be calling in a case of dire emergency. But then they remembered that you had arrived and their panic, if not irritation, softened to indulgence and finally warmth. If I pressed you on this now I am certain you would not even recall it, so taken were you with the meadow and the scattering of macadamia trees that flanked the drive. Out of New York for the first time in your life, you were full of wonder and mischief; running back and forth the length of the meadow with one of the yard dogs from the neighboring farm, each trying to exhaust the other, pulling yourself up the first trees you had ever climbed that were not in Central Park and swimming the river that divided the house from the village, not minding the rain or mud, nor the stones on the river bank and bed that bruised and cut your feet.

– I'm looking for work. Anything you have.

– Can you build a fence? Knock down a wall?

– I've little experience, but I can try. I'm strong and can work hard. Been asking at the other farms, but they're having the same problems as those I left behind in the city. All of us, scrabbling around like mice.

The bulk of my work, what they will remember, sprang from those words. You; sitting on the veranda steps while I fetched you some water, returning to see how the light treated your face; how everything changed during that minute I was in the house.

On those first afternoons I sketched you, you were restless, wanting to be anywhere but indoors. Instructed to keep your eyes forward, you constantly deviated, looking past the window to the garden table where Vishni had promised you that she would serve all meals. Those twin pulls have never changed: someone to put home-cooked food in your belly and the need to feel your feet in the grass. This is why I know you can never leave, not entirely. Something will always bring you back. Inside and out, you have made roots here; from pushing your fingers deep into the earth when you thought no one was looking, as if the feel of soil between your hands and under your nails made it real; and from your face being in the paintings. Whether you are aware of this or not, you have created invisible roots capable of dragging back the unwilling. Once they are unfurled they will recoil. In the meantime I have my work to keep me occupied and the smell of Vishni's coffee burning on the hot plate to jolt me when my attention slips.

We are husband and wife. Some run a shop or diner together. This is ours.

You once said that the darkness of the studio was my comforter, having watched my first minutes or so there each morning, when I seem wrapped up in its closeness before rolling back the shutters from the skylight.

– It's like the dark is some kind of magnet. Pulling away all the shit that's amassed since you were last here. Everything about you is different. Another person.

In those days you were referring to a myriad of things. Attention, wanted and unwanted; the demands that often pulled us away from work. Now our problems are more localized, to do with ageing bodies and various worries about the condition of the house. We have both had recent spells in hospital, which each will not talk to the other about; the magnet's main area of concern. You were amazed that I could cut off mid-sentence as soon as I reached the studio door; how my face would change, the hold it had on me. It is true that the moment often feels like a shrug, something similar to walking through disinfectant before diving into a municipal pool, or the long, measured exhalation of a yogi's asana. I need this ritual in order to feel ready; precious seconds to right wrongs and clear my mind. The day ahead feels unbalanced if I do not begin by walking into black.

Vishni's sixes and sevens have rubbed off on me. I stand in darkness for longer than I should, imagining the lump of rags on the floor to be your prostrate frame, twisted into the shapes I long made you hold. I have often started the day without you being in the studio. This part is normal; a series of corrections and progressions that can be made without the model present. There may have been many periods of days, months even, when I wished for it to be more that way; when the sound of your voice riled me, or simply the sound of mine. If only then I had the ingenuity, the confidence to believe that working alone from a mere set of photographs rather than using a sitter, could reveal a truth. But I needed you. If you were not here to start, at my request or otherwise, you were always nearby: somewhere in the house or on the land. At your most petulant you still responded to my call when it came. You had various stages of wonder and resentment of the process, sometimes hating it to the point where you were ready to happily destroy the paintings, but still you came when I called. Your claim to this room, where you have stood every day for the past fifty years, is greater than mine. I gave my eyes, but you readily gave up your soul. And again. And again.

You are coming back. I know it. You are probably minutes away. The work can continue. Vishni's fears shall be allayed. But still I stand at the door, unable to move closer to the painting. Do you remember how I told you about the house I was raised in, how there were crucifixes in every room, but that the largest one was above my parents' bed; terrifying in its expansive iron cast, the face writhed in pain so lifelike, the gaze itself inexplicably direct, that as children we were unable to go past that room without breaking into a run, so determined were we not to look at it. Without realizing it, we trained ourselves to look downward whenever we were in that part of the house, because to catch even the briefest glimpse of His tortured face frozen in acceptance would be to turn to stone. Many summer days were cast over for one or other of us by making that mistake. It was only later that I understood what my mother must have gone through, having to make love and give birth on that bed with a grotesque Christ hanging over her. This wasn't an icon of a loving God, but something else entirely: a wedding present from my paternal grandmother who disapproved of the marriage. And slowly something from that face seeped into our general behavior. We still ran around and played like other children with our mischievous, secretive ways, but in the house, at table and before our parents, we were mostly quiet, our heads often bowed. My father put this down to God-fearing, from his teaching and that of others, and was pleased. It was once I had left home, that I retrained myself how to see, how not to be afraid to look at the face of anything, that the act of looking propelled me like no other. And when he saw my first paintings exhibited he understood that it was not God that I was ever fearful of, merely the propaganda that dictated the Art around Him. He could not bring himself to comment, or even come close to me, only to seek out the gallery owner and shake her hand before leaving. That was the last of my work he looked at. He never saw my paintings of you. I haven't thought of my father in a long time, but seeing the easel now shrouded in half-light, the back of the canvas facing me, I am reminded of him and of the crucifixes. How I cannot bring myself to look at the painting as it was left yesterday. Essentially, it will appear no different than it was the day before, but I will start looking for cracks, a gesture in your eyes or hands I might have unwittingly captured that explains where you might be. Was the river in your eyes? The beach? What was it I missed that now prevents the painting being real? What have I been looking at, if not you?

And it is that fear above all others which keeps me from the easel: that I have seen something with false eyes, added something that was never part of you. I have left work unfinished before. All around this room are canvases of ideas that have not worked, missteps that cannot be repaired. Everything starts with past failures in mind. It is one of the cornerstones I work from. For those paintings that navigate beyond that, the finish point is to be satisfied that I have done everything I could and no more. For the moment, I cannot decide where this current work sits. Your absence makes the decision ominous. All I can do is take the blanket from the floor, where you were sitting last night, and throw it over the easel, at last shrouding your face and neck. Only your hands are visible, crossed in your lap, your index fingers pointing outward as if in the direction of what went wrong.

I AM LYING ON the daybed when Vishni appears for a second time. She came earlier, tense in her posture; the oxygen tank pulled closely behind her frame, as if I could not hear the creak of the trolley that carried it. The clumsiness made me angry and I sent her away before I could taste what was actually needed: slow inhalations of sweet gas to give me strength and clear my mind. They say I should use it as often as needed. I ration that advice and its practice; hateful of both. Sleep will not come, neither work, but by now I have opened the skylight and placed a sketchbook on the small table next to me, knowing that pencil can be more comforting than paint. Even without you the day must end with progress being made. Vishni's face is dappled by patches of light breaking through the cloud; something from both this and the coyness of her gaze make her appear ten years younger. It makes me think about one of the pictures, labored over beneath this skylight, now hanging in one of the ambassadorial residences: Helsinki or Buenos Aires. At this age, not every work I remember, and this rarely troubles me. Lists and chronology are best left to collectors and other documentarians. When I do remember, especially if the work was good, it is mostly worthwhile. I think of the sweat, the processes and the mistakes. The fear of not knowing what I was doing, of falling into an abyss of banal movement, can be looked upon with fondness. In those days

11

I was always so quick to be angry with myself. Nowadays I still hold myself to task, but I have learned to be more forgiving. These are not the hands or eyes of a twenty-year-old, or forty-year-old. I have learned to work with what I have. Vishni's posture is similar to now, bent forward and conspiratorial, momentarily glancing backwards at the door, wary of being overheard.

– Who's here?

– Ben. He said not to disturb you if you were busy. He's on the porch, reading the newspaper.

– But why is he here? He usually calls beforehand. I didn't hear the telephone.

– You asked me to disconnect the phone last week. The hospital chasing the appointment you missed.

– Tell him I'm working. I can't see him now. Ask him to stay and have lunch with John. They always find things to talk about.

– He's not back yet.

– He's not back? Can you give Ben some lunch anyhow? He's more likely to leave once his belly's full.

For a moment you had become one of the old paintings: your absence forgotten. And then to suddenly remember, like the shock of waking from a sudden sleep; chest beating with guilt. Vishni will not be fooled for long. Her face is studious as I recover myself, processing every gesture. She has learned too many of my tricks. Alone, I open the sketch-book and shape some lines from memory. You, leaning over the fence toward the meadow, pondering a comment you made to which your walking companion, Ben, is laughing heartily. I have always admired that about you: your ability to make strangers feel welcome, not just to do with hospi-tality, but with ease. You are always comfortable, unshaken, willing to be open with everyone. I remember how you charmed and subsequently became brotherly with those

12

stubborn farmers who refused to sell us firewood because of how we were dressed, and also disarming the ladies who gossiped at the store. They are still untrusting of me on my rare trips to town, my demeanor varying from hesitant to brusque in my inability to make even a chink in their stony faces, but you they have time for. You have become like family, celebrating the birth of their children, their marriages, and paying your respects at the burial of their dead. My friends from the city too, when entertaining here was as important as work, all initially suspicious, waiting for you to trip yourself up with your story, until they realized that they loved you more.

That afternoon with Ben was languid; the midsummer heat imbued you both with uncharacteristic sloth while I carried on working at the back of the house. Your masculine laziness was a wonderful thing to see: burnished, and in Ben's case sunburnt, limbs stretched over chair arms and the edge of the kitchen table once lunch had been cleared. You drank beer with lemonade and read each other the oddest classifieds you came across in month-old editions of the *New York Times*, which Vishni saved to wrap up food for the trash. Patti Labelle and the Bluebelles were playing on a low volume, Ben joining in on 'I Sold My Heart to the Junkman' because, as he kept telling you, a girl had once sung it into his ear as they made love. You played dominos and waited for me. Boyish laughter rang through the house making me want to leave my work and join you. The piece I was working on was somehow dead in my hands in the face of so much life outside my door. You and Vishni often laughed together, giving the front of the house a lightness the back lacked. But there was something different, more vital in this chorus of masculine joking. It pounded deep inside my head and groin, intense and pleasurable.

I was reminded of being a teenager in Jersey Heights

and sitting on the promenade railings with groups of boys, pulsing with the joy that comes from seeking attention but also fearing its strength when it finally came. However much I wanted to crash your boys' party, though I was aware that you were both waiting on me – that the shape of the day was dictated by my needs and working patterns, and how powerful that made me feel, made overt by a thumping in my chest – I could not intrude on your intimacy. You had the closeness of siblings, the way you shared the pitcher of spiked lemonade and bickered over whose turn it was to get up and flip the record. You talked about everything but me; the World Series, whether a horse can belch, the women in Hawaii. Paintings were the business of both of you and these were never mentioned. It was an unspoken rule between you. Outside the studio we all talked about other things. There were too many other things to talk about. A mixture of longing and envy kept me going through the day. Also, stubbornness, because I didn't want either of you to think I was cutting my day short on your account. You were young men with egos. You would have dined off it for weeks. When I finally had done all I could, on a painting that was going nowhere and shortly after abandoned, I joined you. I planned on playing the martyr for your simple amusement, and to prove to myself that I had not been forgotten. Dinner was close to being served but you were nowhere near the table, instead fooling around at the paddock. By now the pair of you were softly drunk, taking it in turns to feed vegetables to the donkey you had recently rescued from one of the farms, where his age deemed him ready to be made into animal feed or glue. The wonder of this as yet unnamed pet illuminated your face. Ben's too. You were as timid as children as you patted him and stroked his face. Other men, similarly inebriated, would have taken it in turns to ride him or some other juvenile cruelty. But you were both cowed by its docile nature and the depth of feeling that seemed to emanate from its lowered eyes. The beast, still wary but sated, moved his head away from the carrots, radishes and celery after a time, preferring instead to nuzzle your fingers. As you turned with delight to share this with Ben, the light hit the side of your face and your neck. You were bronzed and smooth, flaxen and happy; it was as if the last days of young manhood were making themselves known. I was blinded by the beauty of it, from the way you smiled to the trail of mosquito bites on your lower arm and the redness of your lips from all the beer. Ben was boyishly loud in his exclamations, vital and alive. I wanted to shout at you both to hold your pose because something from that moment needed to be kept. You were perfect. But I held my voice, because to explain it would be to kill your naturalness. You did not need to be made aware of how the sun had blessed that seemingly random moment and made it golden. Maybe you were both aware that something special had occurred, that had nothing to do with light or Art, but only with friendship. My visions of your impending age were not to be shared; wishing for crow's feet to form and a coarseness in your hair's texture to emerge so that I would have more to work with; that in my impatience for your youth to fade I was willing your decay. It was left to Vishni, whose voice carried overhead, calling us to the table while berating the boys for feeding the vermin what had been set aside for the salad.

THOUGH BEN AND I spoke regularly, we had not seen each other for over three years. I was not ready to hold another show and he had other artists to attend. The Thanksgiving parties we held at the house were a thing of the past, and neither you nor I were particularly keen to spend the summer roasting in his clapboard house in Provincetown. Your remark after one of Ben's many invitations arrived (Independence Day gathering, Memorial Day gathering; an endless list) never left me.

– Beach parties hold nothing for you. Me neither. I can't see you wearing funny hats and sipping on Rob Roys with sand up your ass. The fire will be the only thing that keeps you there; how it moves and what it shares.

You could be overly protective then, taking pains to avoid those social events where I might be expected to sing for my supper. Ben's entertaining never quite fell into that category, but his address book was a varied one and even in the most informal setting, an expectation to perform could still be felt. Your smart-aleck comment perfectly described my feelings toward seasonal laziness, though something in what you said only rang half-true. You were born and raised on the banks of the Hudson. When you felt suffocated and near violence, from arguing parents and the high, airless rooms of your cramped apartment, you jumped the subway to the Ellis Island ferry, where you looked out at the Atlantic. Being close to expanses of water, ocean waves rolling and crashing far beyond the horizon, rebalanced your shaken equilibrium and helped to make sense of your half-formed world. But you rarely spoke of it. They were stories that occasionally came out while I was painting; fragments of a past life that were left for me to piece together. A father, a brother in the navy; connected stories told years apart. When we traveled to London for my first retrospective over twenty years ago, we took almost all our meals at a restaurant you found near Chelsea Bridge. I took for granted that you wanted to look across the river at the landmarks, not realizing your interests were more localized than that; the trail of solitary rowers that passed, the water lapping the bank at our feet. Back home, the stream wasn't directly in sight from the porch, a meadow and a dip in the hill away, but we could hear its gentle rushing as we ate; opened our windows and allowed it into our bedrooms at night, its hypnotic quality more powerful than the ticking clock in lulling us to sleep. In London, your anxiety was such that, at your instigation, we changed hotel rooms several times and then finally the hotel itself, until we found one that gave the view of the water that you desired. At the time, your basis for complaint was due to noise, how you didn't want my sleep disturbed by the roar of traffic and passers-by. I had several important meetings with museum trustees, interviews with newspapers and dinners with long-standing patrons cultivated through Ben. You wanted me to be as relaxed as I could be under the circumstances. But now I see how agitated not being near the water made you. You were on edge for much of the trip. We argued constantly. Could I have taken the sting out of our frozen winters by accepting some or all of Ben's invitations? What internal development was halted by keeping you away from the sea? What was it about these things that you cannot bring yourself to explain?

– You look tired. Have you not been to bed?

I feel Ben's moisturizer rub off on my cheek as we kiss. The scent of something tropical lies thickly between us, the bitter intensity of lemongrass, mixed with citric acidity. As ever, he is immaculate; although he looks after artists, he is not interested in looking like one. This never brings out any self-consciousness about my own appearance, only a reminder that a more refined presentation exists for those that have the energy to invest in it. If anything, his narrow-fitting suit tailored in New York by English expatriates and shirts with their thick navy stripes, his pastel linen shorts cut above the knee and Breton tops are another kind of uniform. Your clothes were different, far removed from city fashion; most often an overcoat one of the farmers gave you. Yet the two of you together still look like kin.

He tries again, his eyes gentle with teasing:

– Getting a little old for all-nighters, aren't we? Seventy-five is when you start to behave.

– I was old when I did them first time around. Now I'm a fossil with a paintbrush.

– Vishni's making her chicken and potatoes with saffron. I forgot how the living's good in the country.

– So long as we can still afford saffron. The kitchen will fall into a slump otherwise.

– John's out, I hear?

– I sent him into town for paint. I think he had some other errands too. He lets things accumulate.

– You should have let me know. I could have brought whatever you needed from the city.

– Almost everything we need is here.

– Let me rephrase that: I would have asked you if there

18

was anything you wanted had I been able to get through on the phone. After two days of getting the busy signal I actually called the phone company to check whether there was a fault on your line. When they told me that it was more likely that you had disconnected the phone I didn't know what to think. It's never bothered you before, has it? And considering so few people have your number; I couldn't understand the reasoning behind it.

His eyes shine with no let up. His lips redden, making the promise of their rosebud shape real; then the red spreads across his cheeks, as the blood rises through his face. The wisps of air that trail his last sentences suggest an exhalation of something that had been saved up since that time: frustration, bewilderment, worry. Ben is Manhattan-bred, used to having his questions answered. An open-ended mystery is fine for the work, but outside of that, there needs to be a concrete order of things. The artists he best represents are those who do not live their lives in total chaos; itself an exaggeration left for those of poorer talent who are only appropriating the role.

– I thought about sending a telegram but was wary of its theatricality. Drawing you out from wherever you were with the painting. A four-word missive from New York, designed to jolt you to your senses. A joke and a nuisance rolled into one, delivered by a sweet-natured, breathless boy, whom you would have to tip handsomely for cycling all this way. I knew you would despise the rigmarole as much as me. That you would hold it against me once the paintings were finished. So the easiest thing was simply to take the train and deliver the message myself: Plug your telephone in!

– It wouldn't happen that way. We're too old to be holding grudges.

– You're also too old to be turning yourself into a hermit,

Anna. The telephone's never bothered you before. You have all the solitude you want out here, without these gestures.

– Takes too much energy, gripes and feuds. It should be left with the young where it belongs.

– Do you understand how people can worry if they don't hear from you, are unable to contact you?

– People, as you call them, know where to find me. I'm always here. As for those that care, two of them are in the house as we speak. The other is buying paint.

– I also hear that you're not taking the oxygen as you're supposed to.

– I have as much as I need. Ignore what you hear.

Ben pours tea and holds out a cup. I take it, well aware that I am still glaring at him; understanding also the heat generated in my body as I bat his invasiveness away. Something in our altercation makes me feel more alive than I have been for these last few hours in the studio. Always the boys who tap my spirit; one at the table, the other buying paint.

THERE IS A SOFTENING over lunch; the saffron that colors and infuses the chicken and potatoes mellows me somewhat, until I feel as light and flyaway as one of those dark-red threads of spice. We share the wine that Ben has brought from one of his father's vineyards, and he talks happily about what is happening with his other artists. He knows, as I do, that there is no sport more torturous than gossip relating to the heightened work rate and success of other artists. In my younger days, those that felt like being under an apprentice-ship of sorts, such talk would drive me from the table, so sensitive was I to the perception of my work and how it measured up to others'. Now there is something pleasant about its buzz. I swat it toward and away from me as if playing with a fly. As insects are a reminder of the summer seasons, so too is Ben's talk, reminding me of the existence of other artists in the world. Jealousy can be just as deeply felt at this age as any other. You of all people understand how jealous I can become. What kills this is ultimately down to personal resources. Energy is finite, and you have to decide how to spend it wisely. Working on canvases taller than either of us, the strength to push a rolling ladder, or climb up the scaffold, can take everything I have. Time spent mulling over profes-sional jealousies would deplete everything.

– Are you going to show me the canvases? It's half the reason I came here.

– What happened to my welfare? You were concerned about so many things.

– That was on my list too.

– Wouldn't you rather say hello to the donkey first?

– I'll feed the old boy his favorites before I go. Let's see some paintings.

– Nothing's ready, Ben. I'm not prepared.

– That's not what I've been hearing from other parties. They suggested you have several ready to go. That it's been the case for almost a year.

– And how do you get to hear from other parties, I wonder? This house might not be clapboard like your place in Provincetown, but the walls are just as thin. I can hear when the telephone rings, as hard as they try for me not to.

– Like I said, there are other ways besides the telephone. He sends letters from the post office. Collects mine from there too.

I think about where you must keep those letters. I would never search your room, but something tells me that they are not in the house, that you probably throw them away as soon as they have been read, the way you do with other more mundane correspondence that reaches the house. Maybe even in the trashcan outside the post office and store. You are agents, of a kind. Your friendship works independently of me, which is how things should be. So why does it jar so, this desire to know what you have been writing?

– Show me. Just the ones you're happy with. Bring them out. Take me to the studio. Anything.

I try to visualize what Ben will see; what the paintings will make him say, how he will feel. I think of your responses when each of the last pieces was finished. The sigh that came from your mouth; something that could be read as a mixture of wonder and satisfaction. Equally, of disappointment. It is not Ben's dissatisfaction that holds me back. I will drag him by the wrist to the studio if I am guaranteed that reaction. It is something that I already feel about my work of the past few years. Disappointment I can understand. I live with it, working daily on canvases that resolutely do not bend to my will, capturing the light differently to what I see. My fear is that he will love it. That he will see the larger works and feel that you are in the room; that the real essence of you, your quietness and sense of wonder about the world, has been made permanent. It will make me question what is deficient in his eyes, and again, in mine. What is it that Ben sees, what insight does he have, what has he shared with you that makes sense of these pictures. That I am capable of capturing something I no longer recognize.

– We'll have to eat some fruit first, otherwise Vishni will be angry with us.

Vishni stands on the kitchen steps holding a bowl of quartered peaches and a jug of cream. Who knows how long she has been there, studying us in our reverie, both light-headed from the wine, induced to sloth from the crisp potatoes. Neither of us seems aware until the moment that our plates have also been cleared away and dirty glasses replaced with fresh ones. I am incapable of seeing anything, I want to tell Ben. Vishni is the one who sees. But I do not want him to leave thinking I am in a depression, because that will only come back to you from another letter left at the post office. Instead I do as I'm told and eat the dessert placed before me, listening as Vishni scolds Ben that he is not eating enough.

– Try either of those jackets on the chair. Perhaps the darker one. It looks like it will be a better fit across the shoulders. Yes? It's comfortable? Right, let me see your shirt. Stand by the window there, please. It doesn't work together. There's too much fuss with those stripes. Sorry, Ben. It's a beautiful shirt, just too distracting. It doesn't work . . . How about something a little softer . . . there's a blue here, or white. The white would be perfect, I think. Unless you would be happier in a color? There's a purple T-shirt on the shelf but it will drain your complexion. What was that phrase you used to tell us they drummed into you at art school: 'We add, not subtract'? There you go; algebra in action. You're about the same size so it shouldn't feel tight on the collar. Oh, whatever you prefer, but maybe the top button open, and also the one after that. Let me see. Two buttons are definitely better than one . . . but not three. That'll be too much.

We are in the room behind the kitchen where Vishni does the laundry twice a week. I cannot bear to take Ben into your room, so pulling the clothes nearest to hand is safer. Your scent is not here, the overwhelming smell of detergent banishing all ghosts. We have swum together in the past, shared a bed for sleeping purposes more than once, making Ben not embarrassed to change in front of

24

me. He has posed before, of course, many years ago, shortly after we first met and before the appearance of you. Ben's painting was one of the first that got me noticed, but you know all about that; what attention does. It is this past history combined with his taste for Provincetown nudist beaches that has schooled him in his lack of self-consciousness. I am sifting through the pile of clothes that Vishni has ironed, looking for further options, so at first I miss an opportunity to note the differences in his body to yours, bar the firmness of his stomach suggesting his continuing loyalty to calisthenics. As he turns around, I see more: the muscular V of his back, the square-packed shoulders and how, despite being as tall and rangy as you are, there is neatness to his frame. He seems so compact. Time is etched on his face, of course, and clings with honor to his neck, but the body is a monument to someone decades younger. He remains smooth and mostly hairless, the other marked contrast to you. Something about his physicality and yours marks you as family, one from either end of blond's spectrum. Ben is dressed, still in his Italian trousers, but the rest is yours, a white T-shirt instead of the shirt, and your navy fishing jumper. I don't know how this is chosen, but somehow we both gravitate toward it, hanging from the door hook. You have worn it for years. Sacred clothing. I think about the darker recesses of the studio, areas where the light does not reach: in the corner opposite the sink, where one frame leans against another; the shelved recess that houses the paint. I think about Ben standing there and how, with his face turned away from me, it could almost be . . . We are both aware of it. His posture changes in your clothes. Now he slouches against the wall, hands in pockets barely wide enough to hold credit cards. Nothing about this is caricature. He is not making a joke as he curves his shoulders inward, lips pursed, arms loose and gangly as if an overgrown boy. He wrinkles his nose.

– This stinks.

– He went fishing last week. You were the one who pulled it down. When he hangs it up there Vishni knows not to wash it. It's one of the quirks he has.

– Doesn't he just! What was he fishing? Are there still trout in the river?

– Brown trout. He has to go where the river passes town these days. Further away from the hills as less seem to travel upstream. He did pretty good last week, though. We were eating for a couple of days.

– Worth coming back for? It's been a while since we went fishing.

– Worth coming back for. You know he'll be only too pleased to take you.

– Maggots running everywhere, plenty of beer drunk, but not much fish, as I recall.

– He's better at it, these days. Has the patience, I should say. You've got a good month or so ahead of you, if you want to take him up on the offer.

– So his letters suggest. Our boy's become quite the country sportsman.

– Something of that kind. Are you going to be happy in that jumper, Ben? You realize that once I start you'll need to keep wearing it.

– That I am aware of.

– And that we won't be able to wash it, less we lose any of the marking?

– I can overdo the cologne to compensate. This is how you want me, isn't it? I can see it in your face. Your eyes are lighting up.

– They are not.

– I know your game. The observer doesn't want to be

looked at, ad nauseam. Well, tough luck! We're going to be staring at each other for a while.

– Not if I have you looking down at the floor.

– And you will, too! Now I understand why some of your subjects were posed the way they were. That little nugget never made it into the notes, did it?

– Stop teasing, Ben. We need to make a start if you want to catch your train tonight.

– I thought I might hang around. At least until John gets back. Shoot the breeze. If he's only in the city, he shouldn't be too much longer.

– I wouldn't have thought so.

– I can take the overnight.

– Don't be silly. Riding the rails through the night like a teenager! Stay over. We'll make a bed up. I'll go and speak to Vishni now because I'm not sure what she had in mind for dinner.

There is an ease with Ben's decision, built on confidence, and from years of having had beds made in countless other artists' residences, from poolside guest houses in California to squats in the wrong parts of London. There are some gallery owners who can barely bring themselves to shake an artist's dirty hand, let alone sleep on a concrete floor; solely interested in the finish. Ben is not one of those. For all the comforts the success of his gallery has brought him over the years, he is still governed by a sense of adventure and an undying fascination in the process. He will spend the night in a tree if he is sure a good painting will come out of it. I hold him still and roll up each trouser leg; tight, narrow rolls that show his ankles. He stops talking now, knowing that he will have ample time to fill during the long studio hours ahead. For now, he is a cipher, who must ready himself to be prodded and pulled. Jumper sleeves are pushed up until they reach the elbow. I point to your shoes that sit by the door.

– Take your socks off, too.

– Sure. Anything else?

– Your jewelry. Watch and ring.

These are slipped off first, but there's something slow in the way he moves now; these last moments where he morphs from friend and house guest to subject. From articulate to voiceless. Even though he still wears his trousers, removing his socks seems to erase the final remnants of who he is. He pulls on the shoes and follows me to the door. His shadow and soft steps are yours.

In the studio Ben moves instinctively toward a row of canvases leaning against the wall. All the care that is given to paintings in the homes they finally end up with is not shared in their places of origin. A sheet protects them from dust, but at various stages they have been handled roughly; marked, nicked in places and painted over. Before perfection – truth – comes digging, dirt. Each canvas bears sign of this excavation, before being hidden by frames and glass. I am a mother bear who carries her cub by the teeth.

– Look at those afterwards. Let's get you in the chair first.

His eyes scan the rows hungrily, calculating how many have accumulated since his last visit. It is clear that he had not expected so many. The eyebrows that frame his widened eyes seem to tremble with the discovery.

– All these?

– Yes. But you can only see some of them. After you've worked for it.

Nodding in affirmation, he moves to the center and waits for me to push the chair toward him. The curiosity for pictures overrides everything, even this house, and his friendship with you. He will not leave without seeing what is under the cloth. Having pushed, dragged back, and pushed again, I motion him to sit. Again, his nod is one of compliance, brisk and sharp, knowing that he will wait patiently, for as long as it takes, until he gets what he wants.

THE EMPTY PLACE set at the table makes the lightness of our dinner talk a fallacy. We sit tightly as if listening to the band on the *Titanic* after receiving premonitions of our doom. The meal is good but there is sadness in the atmosphere, dulling taste buds and tampering with digestion. Ben does his best to play along, his easy manner and ability to keep the conversation going eventually relaxing us, so that at certain moments it feels like a replication of previous dinners, when the room was filled with the simple pleasure of friendship, and the absent place could be explained away by your fetching the wine, the watermelon, the cheese. It is only at the end of the meal, when interest in Vishni's rose cuttings and my redundant gossip about other artists can no longer be tolerated, that Ben's manners evaporate and he becomes testy.

– Why the hell isn't he back yet?
– Soon. I'm sure it'll be soon.
– He should be here by now.

We jump as his hand slaps the table, its echo as hard and flat as his palm. Our eyes meet momentarily before taking them elsewhere, both stabbed with sudden hurt as the realization dawns that you are not there for us. All this had only been a way to pass the time. He has waited all day for you. The world has tilted in your absence. After dinner everyone goes to bed, as if an early night will somehow

30

speed up the process of your return. The table is left uncleared, kitchen detritus left to soak. It is the earliest in years that the house has fallen to darkness. With Ben and Vishni sleeping downstairs, one in the guestroom, the other in her room behind the kitchen, adjacent to the studio, the house feels lopsided. In bed especially, I feel poised to tip; how little it would take to tumble me: a gust from the open window, the telephone's ring. Before I draw the curtain, I stare up at the stars and wonder whether the city's neon would hide the bear and the scorpion from your sight; whether you would use the constellations to guide you from Penn Station to Hell's Kitchen. Remember when you first moved here, you taught me how I could navigate my way home after dark by following the scorpion's tail from rear end to tip? Imagine being born and raised in the country and never having learnt these skills; what a wonder you were! Every day, there seemed to be a wondrous new discovery to be made about you: setting traps behind the refrigerator that caught the kitchen rat, mending windows, your ability to recite any number of poems from *Leaves of Grass* that a well-meaning teacher had forced you to learn by rote as punishment for a litany of youthful misdemeanors. All this on top of the paintings. But navigating the stars was a party trick I never tired of. It was like leaving the world behind for the celestial. You made the walk so often from our country station, nothing grander than a platform and a sign thick with dust; you may as well have been blindfolded.

In the city too, where the steps that lead home are ingrained in your memory, you walk from Penn Station without sight: along Sixth, heading downtown. You pass the fancy shops, virtual museums of aspiration for tourists and office workers, always closed to the likes of you; affordable yet still overpriced; and finally past those less desirable, stores that only stand because it is cheaper to open than shut up completely. Below Avenue A you hit your stride: deep down into the city's unfathomable bowels. Then, nothing. A hinterland of boarded-up warehouses and tenements, long since abandoned, that now shelter only hobos and the spoils of local crime, theft and drugs. Though you are several blocks away from the Hudson, its dank fills your nostrils. You gorge on a nourishing stink that gives your aching muscles life. It is the closest you will get to milk now you are decades past weaning; now that your parents are no longer here to fight over and nurture you. What you are looking for no longer exists, and yet, there you are, standing outside an apartment that is now a laundry, on a street where life as you know it has vanished. I know this is where you will end because it is the one place you have never showed me. I had to find it for myself during visits to the city. A piecemeal search: riding subway lines and roaming every back street until I could be sure. If you feel the weight of the tenements across your shoulders, find some space among the stars. Drop all that you have carried and let the lightness of the night take you. If you are no longer angry, look up and let the sky speak for us. Take your photographs so that clarity comes from your anger. At the very least, one good picture should emerge from the black mist that marks your mourning for everything you left behind. All that you missed, the funerals of your parents, your brother's homecoming, the rapid decline of the tenements, how your neighborhood vanished into a ghost town, will be captured somewhere in the roll of film you carry in your pocket. That is one thing I can be sure of.

– Whatever happens, no matter how long I have to sit in the studio or sand down and creosote the fence? Whether I have to help James birth his dairy cows, or shell a bucket of peas for Vishni, I must take one good photograph a day. Just one. I'm not greedy, Anna. I only want one to lead to another and then the next. It's like crossing the mountain river when we go fishing. You take the pass one stone at a time.

Where did those photographs go? Developed at the drug-store and then placed in a box at the bottom of your ward-robe. Sifting and poring. The bad photographs bundled together and burned with the trash. The examples deemed good sometimes shown to me and Vishni, most often not. You were not secretive but your photos were a private undertaking; something you started over the last few years to make sense of the practice I had committed you to, when you were probably too young to understand what it truly meant. Your interest in photography began shortly after we last saw Ben, a Halloween party high up East, when Provincetown's tourists had long since returned to the city and the cobwebs you had sprayed in all corners, combined with the creaky walnut floors, gave his house a feeling of the *Marie Celeste*. We were a party of eleven almost groping in the dark for other signs of life, the spirits of those who had lived and partied here during that long summer. You and Ben talked alone for much of the night, or that is, Ben spoke to you. Your faces were mostly serious, none of the fooling around that Vishni and I were so used to. His mouth so close to your ear, your neck craning into his, you were a hair's breadth from a kiss. When he remembered his manners as the host, you flicked through the monographs in the upstairs room he used as an office. I found you crouched over his albums, oversized books the size of table tops, filled with giclée prints from artists he was interested in. You were looking at photographs of crumbling diners and abandoned gas stations deep in the country; of families of hobos dressed in found hippy clothes riding the freight

33

trains. The gloss from the prints reflected in your eyes and back onto each plastic sheath that held them.

– They're amazing. Why has he never shown us this stuff before?

– Probably because we never asked.

– All this time it's been sitting in his house. All this time.

In your wonderment you soaked everything up, as you used to do when you first saw my paintings. You still had interest in those, but not the sense of wonder as now overtook you with Ben's photographs. I knew, because something similar had happened to me many years before. I saw a Modigliani portrait hanging in an alcove of a Chicago museum during a college trip and I felt my mind unlock. It has felt as if the last three years has been a slow period of unlocking, of opening yourself up to new possibilities and closing your mind to me. I do not say this from a sense of jealousy. I have often lain awake wondering how this life would ever nourish you, how sitting like a statue day in and out could ever be enough. I took you at your word when you said it was; took heart in how fast your legs ran around the meadow; how rosy your cheeks had become from eating good home-cooked food; the pride you had in being known and respected among the community, whatever they may have thought of me; but most of all because of the trust you had in my hands as they posed you and the nodded appreciation at the end of each day when you saw the progress made on the canvas; how even my stolid snail's pace still felt like some form of magic. You have spoiled me over the years with your patience and blind faith; whether this was something I encouraged in you or that simply lay inert in your personality, waiting to be drawn out. Either way, it has made me fat and somewhat complacent. I was like a suburban wife who believed she was enough for her husband; that he would never stray elsewhere. Now I am

34

suspicious, mistrustful, as she might be after being wronged; bitterness staining her tongue. You have given yourself up so readily and for so long, I don't know how else to be. Your face is puffy with all the secrets you hold, the lining around the eyes tight as you hold them all in. When I am cleaning up I sometimes catch you out of the corner of my eye, staring at the paintings as if you want to burn them. Who planted the seed for that, Ben or I? I move as you do, by stealth, forcing lightness into my heavy legs as I tiptoe across the floorboards so as not to wake those below. The room is dark but never completely black. Black is for those who refuse to see color, even the red of their eyelids as they close. The hook on the back of your door where the camera used to hang is unadorned. I feel it as I push it open, hearing nothing knock against the wood on the other side. For most of the day I had been caught up thinking about your clothes, forgetting that if you left carrying your camera you would have all you need. So much about today has been about remembering and forgetting. The rigor of the studio shields me from the worst of it. Only at night do I lapse. Even as I open your wardrobe and pat my hands along its varnished floor, I know that my fingertips will find no resistance; that your slim box of photographs will be gone. The only picture left in the room should be where it always was, in a frame on your dresser. There were never any paintings here, only this. Still feeling my way, I pat up and around until I find it, hoping that this will have been taken too; that there is room for this one photograph in a stack of many. But as I stand by the window and shake the frame open, I see that it is still there, a happiness you no longer wish to remember; of us in our evening finery taken at the reception in London.

I watch the darkness fade shivering on the porch, wrapped in two of the thickest blankets we saved for winter. I think of the bachelor party they threw for the farmer's son not so many years ago: how the lot of you raised hell over three towns and the outskirts of the city before a chastened return on the first morning train. I remember hearing of you all stumbling down Main Street at sunrise; an army of penitents. And then a memory of you alone, walking with uncertainty through the meadow toward the house. You were benignly drunk, the strengthening sunlight pushing through your greasy hair and making an angel of you. How you slept where I am sitting now, on a love seat no bigger than a cot, because you did not want to wake the house. It is foolish of me to expect you to reappear in the same way, as night rescinds and morning beckons, but I do so. Like a young woman I rehearse how I am going to look and what to say. In reality, of course, we will have nothing to say to each other. A look will pass between us, something that can reassure the other that there is no animosity, and then only sleep, from which your cheerfulness will return.

– You should have seen the size of them. Twenty in all, and of a height to make our farm-bred boys look minute. Fed on bad manners and smog, thighs for arms from all the lifting on the docks. Put one of them next to one of us and we looked as unstable as a skittle. And boy were they ready to knock us down! Didn't like the look of us or the way we spoke. That we could be drunk and still be mindful of our manners. They weren't used to so many smiling faces in that miserable place. I can't recall how we even ended up there, save the neon sign calling us, with its promise of beer and can-can girls. The only thing that saved us getting a beating outside that bar was that our legs were not solid like hams. We could run faster. One of us – I can't remember who, but it could have been me just as easily as the next man – tipped up a table to give us a head start, and we piled through that tiny door and out into the street as quick as we could. We were like anchovies being pulled from a jar; as ungainly. The air was salty, thick with our sweat. The sound of glasses and bottles masked their threats toward us for a merciful few seconds. And in one of those, at least, they were cut silent, the sudden move surprising them more than they could articulate. They had not banked on Hicksville country mice using their wits. We ran through the docks, fast in our pack, pounding hard until our feet were sore and chests fit to bursting with effort. Their voices carried past the few warehouses but their feet didn't follow. They didn't have the energy for it, not when there was still beer to drink, and stony-faced women to heckle. Which reminds me, the neon did not live up to its promise. These were definitely not girls. Faces and necks crisscrossed with lines, powder and lipstick thickly lodged in every crevice; breasts and bellies sagging from bearing children; eyes as dark and hard as flint. They were nothing like the girls we were thinking of, which was a sign of our ignorance of what such a bar should be like. Even though you have made me see things as they really are, when I was with the guys all I could think of was the ideal. How funny is that? The only thing I'm sure of is that you would have wanted to stay if you had come along. You would have painted every single one of them. In the midst of our running, I emerged at the front, escaping that fear I have of being hemmed in, I suppose. I found myself leading the boys past one warehouse after another until I got a rough sense of direction from the lights far up on the Lower East Side glittering on the Hudson. That too became something to run from, another place I only wanted to remember as an ideal. My heart was beating fast, both from the running and the fear that one of the guys would ask why we weren't running uptown, where drinks and girls would be plenty. The double-rush of adrenaline made me feel drunker than before. I was dizzy with it, so light-headed, to the point where I thought my brain would float away, leaving just a pair of running legs and this urgent heartbeat. But nothing was said. We were all overtaken with running; the strength and enjoyment of it. Our feet and breath became harmonized, and if someone had suggested we run all the way home, we were all of the presence of mind to possibly attempt it. Once we left the dockside, uncertainty sat in the air, but I was still at the front, still being followed. I kept my eyes ahead. We passed the factory where my father worked his whole life but I stayed fixed on the street. I didn't turn my head at the chimneys that used to fascinate me as a kid. Nor at the gated entrance where I would wait for him at the end of the day and where the vans delivering raw hides from all over the city passed. I never stopped. They all ran with my fear on their shoulders. Their muscles ached with it. Only as we reached the bridge did I slow, relishing in the boundary before me; knowing that once I was in Brooklyn I could not be touched. I could drink in Brooklyn. Breathe, and be my own man. Feel that he wasn't standing over my shoulder. So I spent the last money I had getting the boys even more drunk and ridding myself of that feeling. With every glass I felt lighter, lighter.

I stayed in the cot and kept lookout.

BEN REMAINS PERFECTLY STILL, though his restlessness shows in his eyes. They roam. Vishni has given him a plate of eggs, followed by fruit; a menu designed to banish tiredness and prevent bloating in morning subjects, and it would please her to see how he ripples with energy. The tremors across his eyebrows crackle with it. He hesitates to speak, not wanting to disturb my concentration, a mood I silently encourage. Unhappy with the previous day's work, I fix him in a variety of poses until I find something I am happy with. The easy chair is dragged back to the corner. Now he is naked on the blanket, lying on his side, his knees pulled halfway toward his chest, as if he is in the process of curling or uncurling; paralyzed by sleep were it not for the strength of his eyes. He makes no complaint about the discomfort of his position. The thin foam mattress under the blanket is deeply pocked in places, so that the floor's chill can be felt. The draft from the open window ruffles his hair and the thin tangle of curls across his prick and balls. At the completion of each sketch, where line and form takes precedence over other details, I have him up on his feet to regain his circulation. I use the exercises that you are so familiar with, and at various times, contemptuous of. Body stretches from top to toe, followed by a couple of minutes' jogging on the spot, as much as my condition will allow. He does as you used to at the beginning, laughing heartily and with some disbelief as I join in with him; someone who notoriously showed little interest in most physical activity.

– So these are your secrets? Why you haven't aged a day?

– Only a fool would fall for that one, Ben. I work, that's all. Just work.

We continue through the morning with a succession of poses and sketches based around the rug. There is no mention of you, as if Ben has made a mental note to learn from last night's petulance. He charms me as if I am an out-of-town buyer in need of flattery. It's something I've always known, the gallery owner's ability to blow smoke up anyone's ass, but something about the silent attention he pays me, the look as tender as an old lover who's parted on amicable terms, makes me think of how artists are as manipulated as buyers. Perhaps more so. That he has offered to strip seems proof. Unless, of course, he wants to look past the sentimental. He knows that my concern lies beyond an obvious search for youth trapped beneath the skin. How I would pay attention to raised veins and the cluster of moles and age spots on his back that cannot be concealed with make-up. The skin tightening into whorls around each temple where his hairline has gently receded. The yellow staining of hard skin on the soles of his feet, the network of veins on the other side, surrounded by deep crevices of soft skin; so that to stare at his feet closely is to see solidified tracks of volcanic larvae. The effect on his hands, too, is that of a life-force spent. Clothed, Ben is vital and alive; but lying there, he is a paradox of strength and weakness: the hard biceps and modest pecs, the hands and feet that give everything else away. With another artist, Ben would be different again. He would play up to the image of Mr Universe by way of California, kissed by the sun gods and still desirable. If the artist was male, there would be flirting, followed by sexual activity. I think of the numerous boys

41

nurtured in Provincetown over the years: highly talented in their various forms, but whose desirability and volatility habitually expired after the first couple of shows. They could not deal with the pressure to produce work, nor the force of their jealousy. Artists and boys are the same to Ben. There is always new talent on the horizon. His loyalty was and is to his women artists, stoic and focused in their work, preferring to be spared the worst of the Manhattan bullshit. He can flatter us in our studios, where seemingly gossamer platitudes are quickly plastered over in paint, clay, or bronze. We can be relied upon to produce; unpredictable in our content, we nevertheless maintain our drive and anger at most things. We are never cajoled the way those boys are, late at night, with drinks and the offer of a permanent bed. We are never beseeched. There are never tears shed, nor heartbreak. And then you: another loyalty that cannot be bought. Your brotherhood is one that would never be put in jeopardy. It is a love grown out of puppy fat, where trust is more important than the need to compete.

– Something tells me this is a picture I won't love. I'll need it, *treasure* it, but it won't be something I want to see easily.

– What makes you say that?

– The way you're looking at me. You're different to how you were yesterday.

– From my usual self?

– You're different, that's all. The way you're holding yourself. The scratch of your brush on the pad. Everything feels harder, more ingrained.

– That's the kind of information you should keep to yourself, Ben. It doesn't work if we're both taking everything in. I don't need to know what you see.

– But this is why I'm so interested! Ten minutes ago I lost the feeling in my left leg, but I didn't tell you, because you were so concentrated, which in itself was wonderful to look at. I'm in agony and I keep my mouth shut because I'm mesmerized by what I'm seeing. Why has no one painted you, as you sit there with your brushes and pad? You'd rather I play dumb and inspect my fingernails or something equally passive, but there was something in that moment just now, in your face, the way the light hit it. If I knew how to take that information and express it through my hands holding a pencil or brush, I would have wrestled that pad from you.

– You're talking like someone who has never seen a painting before. You've been surrounded by artists all your life. The murals in your parents' house, the gallery—

– That doesn't mean anything. I'm talking about your face. What I saw in your face.

– Well . . . that's something I'll have to take your word for.

We stop again briefly and then continue. It is understood that everything now is a cycle of stretching and posing. He drinks cold coffee because there is not enough time to make fresh and I do not want to call Vishni. To open the studio door would be to depressurize the morning's work, which I don't care for. A precious few minutes would be lost in meaningless chat. Even if neither speaks, an additional presence, the weight of her eyes as she scans the room, taking in the details of his position and mine, will batter our equilibrium for a time afterwards, like passing storm winds against a brick house. I am also mindful that although she is not shocked by nudity, far from it, this would be the first time she has seen Ben this way. While he is still a guest, the processes of work are as much about protecting modesty as secrecy. They always were.

Even naked, there is something so composed about Ben that I feel cumbersome in his presence. The small folds of skin under his ankles negates this. The redness of his neck and ears, as a new position forces the blood flow to his head. You used to ask me why I paint, as if somehow I'd never asked that question of myself. I suppose many years ago, long before you, I would have allowed weeks to roll by as I pondered. Unsure as to whether what I was doing gave me any right to call myself a painter. But that was before I'd done much work, and a lot of other things. My eyes were still stinging from the fumes of new paint, my fingertips raw with turps, back aching because I hadn't yet understood how posture was as important as what I saw. When I was pretending to be an artist I asked myself those questions. When I began to work, really work, they stopped.

– I want to paint what I see. There's something else, but I can't explain it. Don't want to.

When you first posed the way I have posed Ben now, there was something so natural about how you lay. You looked as if you had been found. You had lived here for three years and your eyes were glazed with secret knowledge. Everything you had learned through our work sweeping the remnants of your boyhood away. It was all I could do to record that moment, that point you'd reached. Your face would change daily. You were not always so docile, but still I held that particular look in, slowly coaxing it out, carefully with my brushes month in, month out; inch by inch.

44

You spend the night in the park, sleeping deep in woodland where you hope you will not be found. The cypresses stand sentry; the gnarled pine, your umbrella. There will be money in your pocket to cover a night or so at a hotel, for as long as it takes until you are ready to ring the buzzer at Ben's apartment and tell him that you have left. Even if your pocket holds only loose change and your ticket stub from the train, you know of two hotels you can call upon, boltholes we have patronized for years, which will give you a room without hesitation. The bank on Fifth knows who you are, enabling you to draw money the next morning or the one after that and settle your account. You are the most comfortable hobo in New York. The paintings allow you to walk the city in rags with a dollar and three quarters and whatever else you have remembered to take. There is so much for you to fall back on, so much infrastructure created over the years with just a day like this in mind, yet still you prefer to lie on the city's imitation of a forest floor and take whatever nature and passing drunks will throw at you. Your need to acclimatize is all encompassing, knowing that you will drive yourself mad cooped up in a hotel room. You want to hear the city's heartbeat; something that goes beyond the horns of traffic passing outside your window. The catcalls of revelers, the grunt and whine of the garbage trucks are an adjunct to the blood flow, but not the force behind it. Even the Hudson only plays a part. Lying on a bench overlooking the tugboats will not give you what you need. And that location was given much thought. It came close to being in your childhood bedroom with the window pulled up; when something in the city's speech drowned out the shouting happening down the hall. The whistle from the tugs as the boatmen talked to one another, calls across water that sounded like song. On those nights when flesh slapping flesh was more than you could take, knuckles crunching cheekbones and thudding into stomachs, the river's edge was your escape. You could hear the words passed between them, paced from the whistle's blows; a chorus decrying a dishonest coal merchant out by Long Island and the slipperiness of whores. You fell asleep to the sound of their fraternity, where goodwilled parlance ran a tightrope, always moments from an argument. But there is something in the silence of the park that calls you. Lying on the soft ground, the snap of branches, rolls of thunder pushing through your butt from the subway a hundred yards below. It is like being in the eye of the hurricane through which every sound must pass. Your ear crackles with the brush of grass or the laughter from a girl rising from the street. You hear the click of dancing shoes in Harlem, the crack of a liquor bottle being smashed against a wall in the Bowery. Foxes cry out from under shrubbery, as do unhappy women in the privacy of their bathrooms. Along the path a stray dog sniffs for food in the empty garbage cans dotted around the benches. Later he ventures into the undergrowth, hoping for more success, but is too timid to come near you. It's a disappointment. You would have happily fed the dog a couple of franks from the tin you picked up at a grocery store on Lexington. He is a mutt of some kind; one that has other rich seams where food can be claimed. His coat is glossy, eyes dark and bright, his legs long and defined. You wonder about the butchers in the meat-packing district, whether their generosity has kept him in this fine condition. Unwanted ribs, chucks and rotting skirt taken from the pile marked for the dumpster and brought down here. This is not a creature that fights with other dogs in an alley for scraps. His face is too unmarked for that. Equally, it may be attributed to the ladies of the Upper West Side, the women of the house or someone from their staff who brings down the last of the roast, or the steak earmarked for an undeserving husband. He will be fed, and sometimes petted, if there is bravery on both sides. You imagine how he nuzzles against a warm hand whose overwhelming perfume is one of gravy and bread sauce. How, in rare instances, he allows his belly to be tickled. Yet he stays away from you. Somehow you do not fit in this climate of generosity. Something in your scent marks you as an outsider. The wrong pollen has attached itself to your clothes. The park's soil is not packed into the ridges under your shoes. You are not clean or dirty enough. Your lungs have not yet inhaled enough of the city's fumes and smog, therefore everything you breathe out is pure. You smell of age, having more in common with the leaves decaying around you than with his benefactors. Compared to those men and women, your heart rate is low, your breathing, small. There is nothing he can learn from you. No strength to take.

There is no understanding from the creature that his strength is what you need. How happy it would make you to fall asleep with the heart of this animal beating on your chest. The loyalty of man and dog, and the simple pleasure it gives. And through sleep how his sporadic whining would tell you everything you didn't know about the city. All that you had missed. You were lying on the ground, warm and damp, because otherwise you couldn't be sure of where you were. You couldn't trust your eyes. You needed the dog to tell you. But he would not come.

BEN IS BEGUILED, the same as you. After a week he leaves for the city to collect clothes and check on the gallery. He plans to redirect his work to the house for as long as it takes until the painting is finished. A second phone line is arranged for one of the upstairs rooms.

– So the gallery can always keep in touch with me without clogging your line. I'd feel less of a nuisance this way.

– No one rings the house. We don't even know if there'll be a painting. We're just casting off, is all.

– Anna, let me. Please. I live in fear of being a bad house guest.

In waiting, anticipation sweeps the house. Vishni works through a list of jobs she wishes had been completed the night he arrived. From lifting furniture, to beating the rugs in the yard, to the endless possible combination of vase and jug placed on the dresser. She moves like a typhoon, one small touch after another designed to make his room homely. I'm drawn in despite myself, taking the stepladder to hang a pair of thickly lined curtains according to her instruction, and change the lampshade over the bed. Our movement seems faster than usual, our coordination more nimble. I am breathless with the exertion of moving up and down the ladder; chest hot with resentment at the pleasure I feel once I have finished. The room no longer looks like an afterthought; it has the feeling of an actual residence, with its low lamps, washstand and small armchair. Still, I feel overcome with the hot-headedness of a girl barely out of her teenage years at the unfairness of this dynamic: us running around like housewives in preparation for a man. I think of the novels I despised as a child and of the air of expectation that must fill the hallways of houses in commuter towns as wives anxiously await their husbands. You were never fussy about your surroundings, dryness and warmth being all that you needed. Ben is a different creature, and Vishni feels this deeply. She is nervous about all her choices, every refinement. That I spend half the day riding this hysteria is more to ensure she is happy than Ben, though he too is appreciative in a manner that satisfies her worry.

– You have made a prince of me. Flowers, kisses, will never be enough for your thoughtfulness.

Still, flowers arrive the next day while we are in the studio, bountiful and extravagant, and the same the day after that. New York manners. The dinner table groans under the competing weight of roses and food, as one gratitude reflects another.

Your room remains untouched and will do so for as long as you are away. I tell them not to move anything, to venture so far as to even open a window. Even with the sparseness of your possessions, there is a sense of permanence there; in a stark contrast to Ben's, which has all the plushness and thoughtless scatter of a hotel room. If you had meant to close your door and never open it again, something of the composition in the air would have told me. The taking of an extra coat or pair of shoes would have made your intention clear. When Ben takes his coat from the hook, the emptiness is apparent. He is gone but not missed; not physically. The air from the house does not weigh on our shoulders or sit heavily at the bottom of our boots.

One aspect of the improvements was a bother. The man

from the telephone company took up most of the day installing the second line. Ben was yet to return, almost as if he knew how much disturbance it would bring and how I would spend that time seething in the barn once the noise permeated every inch of the studio. Silence is not always conducive to working well, but nor was this singular invasion. When there wasn't drilling and hammering, there was raucous laughter from the kitchen as he made the most of Vishni's hospitality. Once he got the measure of how generously she catered, the delicacy of his work during the afternoon, painfully slow in his line-feeding, tacking and testing, ensured he did not finish until the scent of the cooking pot reached him a second time. The man was from one of the local towns, distant enough that we did not know him by sight, but well aware of the house and its reputation. His eyes roamed freely, looking for stories to take back.

– So this is what it looks like inside, is it? I don't know what I was expecting, but from the way I heard it, nothing this . . . ordinary.

The thickness that ran under his chin and along his gut suggested an innate satisfaction with being born and raised on this fertile soil; no different to those smirking faces at the store. The yearning in his eyes was only for a second chicken leg with gravy rather than for youthful opportunities lost. His legs would not run the way yours did.

– Small room for a telephone. You couldn't find a smaller space if you tried.

– Hotel rooms have phones. Nothing very strange in that.

– True enough. Is that an office they're planning to make there? I could understand why a second phone line was needed if this was an office.

– Stop with the questions and eat your chicken. I was going to offer pudding, but your forwardness is making me have second thoughts.

A pie lay between them, heavy with dusted sugar and threat. The man said no more, finishing his meal with an amused expression, one that would be exaggerated for his co-workers when he returned to head office.

Did you see her? they'd ask in succession, a modicum of interest aroused by the name, as if he was talking of a panther or another rarely seen creature.

– Not a sign. I heard her plenty, belly-aching about the noise. At one point a cup or plate was thrown against a wall that I heard only in the back of my head against the drill. But the housekeeper kept me away from her – or should that be the other way around?

– Did you see any of them?

– No. The walls were bare. Nothing but flowers and brass plates.

The phone line weighs heavily at night. I barely glance at our telephone in the hall, even after Ben reconnects it. I never once imagined that you would use it, so paid it no mind. You are not one for telephones. Every word you speak down the line seems to strip away your intentions: good humor never rings true; your confidence becomes something brash and liable to offend. I can only trust your silence; the sound of your breath in my ear tells me more than anything else you say. Those times when you are away from the house, farm or harvest work, your messages are brief and convivial, aware of an audience around you.

– The calf is stuck. We're waiting on the cow doctor, but if he's not here soon we're going to have to cut her open.

Later you would tell me how you clammed up with farmers and their wives standing over your shoulder; how you felt each word break down into a stutter of consonants. A flare of heat ran from the back of your neck and across the side of your face. You were overwrought with the possibilities of what might happen to the heifer, nervous that your voice didn't give it away. You had birthed before, and shot horses that had gone lame, but something that day cut through any notion of routine; the trembling of the cow and the fact that she did not bellow, but acquiesced to your hands. The farmers required what you had always given: a strong hand and a tight-lipped confidence. The farmhouse hall was not a place where crying should be heard. You called again a couple of hours later, after the vet had failed to arrive (learning the next day that he had driven his car into a ditch and was crossing the valley on foot). There were no words then, just your breathing into my ear, hoarse and thick, and the background commotion of the wives as they were told the news.

– I know.

– I know.

You carried it on as a joke subsequently, wanting to ride over the rawness of that moment; needing it to be stamped into long-forgotten memory. I needed oils from the store, specific reds that you were unable to find. Your silence and a sigh, with the barest hint of theatricality at its edges, told me, followed by a giggle, because we knew then that this would be our language. What passed between us in the studio was now also something real outside of it. Across the other rooms in the house we were no different to how married people conducted their business. We fussed, bickered and held grudges. But from one telephone to another, we were silent, close to heavy breathing like the perverts some in the town suspected us to be. And at night, in our respective rooms, falling asleep to the sound of the other.

We have the new telephone to ourselves for one full day before Ben returns. Vishni rings the store and has them call her back to test its capabilities. Then she polishes the receiver several times. Once she leaves, and later while she sleeps, I sit on the edge of the bed and await your call, as I know it will come. Ben will send you the number, somehow.

– Oh yes, it was him. Of that I have no doubt.

– Did he identify himself?

– There was no need. He was like a mirror image from the moment I opened the door. And if there were any questions, they were put to rest when he stood before the painting.

– He was pleased with what he saw?

– It was as if he had stepped from it. The same haircut and shirt. The shoes had clearly taken some wear, but they were still recognizable.

– He is not a ghost. Just attached to those clothes.

– So I gather. I am not, I imagine, like others who buy your paintings, Anna, in that this was bequeathed by a congregational member to whom I became close. There are neither the funds nor the inclination for work such as yours to reach us otherwise.

– That I understand. We were made aware of the bequest after Mrs McMahon had passed. It's an eccentricity my dealer has, wanting to know where each painting is. A mania that sometimes reaches me. Some of the transit passes through my ears, but yours I remember.

– Not just from your dealer, of that I'm certain. It was a scandal across the borough that such a valuable work should be personally bequeathed this way, with firm instruction not to sell it on behalf of the Church. Many felt I was undeserving; that a painting should not be enjoyed by a person such as me, who has greater moral matters to consider.

– And he spoke to you, Father Michael?

– He had no need to speak. I knew who he was. That painting has hung on my wall for so long, I know every crease in that boy's face. I know the whorls in his eyes, the colors within colors. The rain must have stopped half an hour or so earlier, but he was still wet through when he stood at the bottom of my stoop. His jaw was clenched tight as if to stop himself from shivering; his forehead taut also, so as not to give in to the cold.

– You led him to the painting?

– I took him to the fire so he wouldn't catch pneumonia. I went to fetch a towel and some dry clothes. When I returned he had stripped down to his underwear and was hanging his wet things on a chair before the fire. Only when I returned, this time with tea and some of the supper I had prepared for myself earlier, did I see that he had found the painting.

– Where is it?

– Opposite the fireplace. I wasn't sure that it was a painting suited to such a sparse living room, but to leave it in the hall would have been to dishonor the sentiment behind the bequest. And there was something indecent about having it in the bedroom. So . . .

– How long did he look at it?

– Long enough for the clothes to have dried and supper to have spoiled. He wasn't interested in anything else, you see. Just a sip or two of the tea, and the painting. He accepted my offer of a chair but turned it away from the fire so he could gaze unhindered. He was no longer damp by this point. I keep the rooms fairly hot in this weather on account of my weak chest. It's the only indulgence I have. That and the painting. The way his hair now sprang from his forehead in its thickening curls was cause for my chest to jump. He became even more like the painting as he dried, almost as if he was waiting for the exact point when he'd be able to jump back into it.

– I thought you were a man who did not believe in ghosts.

– The Spirit. But that is something else entirely. Ghosts, if they exist, have no interest in a spartan house in Brooklyn.

– When we have seen the work in private houses, nestled among the decoration, it can sometimes mute the noise that has built up inside while creating it. There's nothing out of the ordinary if he was quiet as he studied it. Elsewhere, in the starkness of a gallery, it's amplified. All your joy and resentment screaming back at you. He can be noisy in galleries for this reason. Talks non-stop. And not only for my work. He's trying to shut out everything else.

– He was quiet, but there were no signs that he was fighting himself. I have seen the faces of the tormented, the weary, but his was not of their number. He was illuminated by it, at once seeming much younger than his years. Curiosity was feeding him rather than unhappiness. He laughed several times. His eyes roamed over every inch of the canvas. The hands were studied at length, then the face and neck. I saw how he took in the brushstrokes that created the parting in his hair and the crook of his raised leg as it rested upon the other knee. I am not an expert in painting, Anna. I can only tell you what I saw.

– You saw everything. You studied him as you would the painting.

– More so, I suspect, once I had taken in what was happening. He is not a visitor I expected to receive. I welcomed him as I do all comers to this house. Those in need are always helped. But my nerves were shot to pieces. It was the shock of seeing his face. There was whiskey put in his tea to warm him up some more; I took a swig or two myself while I was making it, because I wanted my expression to imbue comfort rather than what was actually there. I caught sight of myself in the glass as I was getting the teacups. I looked terrified.

– You were frightened of him?

– A man arrives on your doorstep without a word? Crosses your threshold without a word? A stranger who is somehow not? Who now stands silently before an image of himself? Almost naked? These are fearful matters. I started speaking for him, filling the room with words until they rose with the heat and settled on my shoulders. I asked how he found me, or how he even knew where the painting was, so long had it been since it was first sold. I was thinking of how tucked away this parish is, for a stranger, and wondered over the steps taken to journey here. But you have answered me on that point; unlike him, who continued to say nothing. He nodded in thanks for the drink, though the whiskey was not noted, as if liquor meant nothing. But his was not the hardened face of a seasoned drinker. His skin was too clear for it. There was a luminescence across his cheekbones and under the eyes, an effect I had often thought must have been exaggerated for the painting, only now I realized that you simply painted all that you saw. The damp flushing of his cheeks heightened it, but it was undeniably there. Everything I said fell into background noise.

– You make it sound like a religious experience. A portrait of a man sitting on a chair.

– I fear you will mock me if I refer to a state of grace, but there was something of that peace in the moment. This vocation, with the Lord's help, teaches you to recognize when people have found what they were looking for, temporal or otherwise. Mine will not come until the last. I've always known it. There is no drive toward an object or place to give me peace. I am not so lucky. It's what makes me acknowledge the fact when I see it in others.

– Did you explain how you felt? That for a man selling faith, you had none of your own?

– How astute you are. To speak so briefly with a person and yet somehow know them.

– I do not have your gifts. It is simply what you have already told me.

– There was no opportunity for a mutual exchange of secrets. He had yet to say a word. I realized that, although I knew his name, I was wary of using it; as if to say his name aloud would make real all that he wished to hide. If he had wanted to offer something tangible, to make something solid of his identity, he would have opened his mouth when he was on my doorstep. He would have shaken my hand. He wanted to be this recognizable stranger, so that the next day it would feel like a dream. Painting aside, there would be no words to anchor him to this place. Except . . .

– Except what?

– There were some things he couldn't keep to himself. The warmth from the fire weakened his resolve. Once he lay on the couch, he slipped. Spoke as if I wasn't in the room, as if to himself. Words that couldn't make sense to a stranger. 'They'll say I've run, when they hear about it afterwards,' he said, 'not knowing that I've seen death. That I'm unafraid of it. She knows that too, if she thinks hard enough.'

– So he did speak.

– That is what I'm trying to tell you. He clammed up when he saw I was paying attention, and dried himself. Later, after an hour or so of standing, he lay on the couch and regarded the painting from there. 'You can see it in my face, can't you?' he said. 'How much I believed that this was the way to live your life.' Only then did his anguish show.

58

THE CAGE WHERE ORLA, the postmistress, sorts the letters is at the back of the building far behind the post office counter, bypassing two trolleys – one broken, one working – and a sizeable pile of gray burlap sacks. The rack spans the full length of the wall, envelopes and packets folded into their chicken-pen compartments. The cumulative effect is of a concertina stretched to its fullest, as a thick band of white from the bundled envelopes runs from corner to corner. The sheer amount of post housed there puts paid to the myth that this town of farms and the two villages beyond it is not the home of letter writers. How many envelopes there contain bubbles of gossip to be passed from house to house? Packets that float to the top of each individual pile and take precedence over bills and other indicators of financial woes. These nuggets seem destined for every address except ours, because I am still considered an outsider who rarely socializes. Under the cages sits a green metal box, twice the size of the compartments, its door held securely with a tarnished brass padlock.

– She gets the letters from there. Watch how she does it when I ask.

Ben talks as he does at parties back in New York, behind a thick smile, in a lowish tone under his breath.

We are the only ones here aside from Orla, having waited at the door on the dot of nine for her to open, and still he

59

speaks this way; a permanent sense of caution governing his habit. That he should be so charming yet always discreet in his actions and never overheard. Orla will be hard-pushed to catch any of our conversation, however much she may want to. Ben asks for airmail envelopes, which sends her running into the back room, and once again, when he also remembers postcards. His smile is ample to negate the resentment that would ordinarily rise in her chest, so that when she returns her cheeks are still pale and not flushed with annoyance. Her mouth is smoothed out from the tight pursed lips I'm accustomed to seeing on those occasions I visit the store alone. In the time we have the place to ourselves, I gaze at the cages and then the metal box without having her eyes on me. It's here that you collected your letters from Ben; missives casually slid between the milk cartons and the heavy cream bought from the general store across the street. Did Orla wonder at the nature of the letters, at why they could never be packaged with the others and left to the mailman to deliver? Or did she count it as one eccentricity among many radiating from our house? You can be forgiven this quirkiness, carrying boxes of enve-lopes to the back of the storeroom without being asked and unloading pallets to her instruction when her afternoon boy fell sick. I could never be granted the luxury of breezing into the post office and asking for the held letters without being judged. It never would have remained a secret anyhow. One way or another, you would have been told. It's a reality I rarely think about, but being either here or in the general store always puts me in this frame of mind: petty and defensive. Tightness pulls the entire length of my spine. As I raise my chin to meet her stony eyes, I feel it all the more. The store does not make me nervous, but there is something I can't identify that sits in the base of my stomach, bringing back memories of Father's farm and its plane trees, and the steps leading up to the clapboard church where we had been baptized and schooled; a place where I felt small and prone to past failures being commented upon. Orla doesn't do this herself; she simply allows the other customers to speak their mind without intervention. Ben is gallant but he is not the protector you were – are. With you there is no other way I could feel but safe, and guarded. Ben's interjections would mean nothing if one of the girls from the mill rounded on me for one of the paintings that had made the newspapers.

– You had her legs splayed like she was fowl bound for the oven. Where's the art in that? Art is the trees around us, the beauty of our land. You made that woman look fallen. There was no life in her. That wonderful woman who cooks and cleans for you and takes all our criticism of her employer with good humor and a degree of feigned ignorance. This is how you repay her work – making her look like that? That a newspaper should print that image, let alone someone buying it for all those dollars is a disgrace. I'm ashamed that you live here. That our town is associated with the sickness in your eyes.

You nodded sharply after she had spoken, before you talked her down. Your words indicated that you respected her right to have an opinion about the painting, but that a personal attack of this sort was not the way to express it. That in nature you could witness all manner of things that had little to do with beauty, but to do with the seasons, the food chain and the need to procreate. How this painting was part of an ongoing project with Vishni. That she had already been the study of many paintings and would continue to be so, much the same as yourself. That it is not the responsibility of Art to draw our attention to beauty, for our eyes are drawn to it anyway, in a myriad of forms.

The woman's mouth continued to open and close in

protest. She did not want to be treated as a pet that needed to be tamed. But as you spoke her face involuntarily knotted in concentration as her anger abated. Your words were leading her back to the paintings most often talked of – you standing in the barn doorway – a politician's wife had bought on behalf of one of the public libraries. How the pride of the community was based on the strength and honesty in your face; only to be forgotten, because it was what happened in the day-to-day that mattered, not a slab of dried oil on canvas that hung in a far-off hallway or reception room. It was amazing how you managed to bring her through that cycle so that once you had finished she was chastened and ready to apologize, but only to you, because she was ashamed of your gentle disappointment. A curt nod in my direction was meant to clear things.

Another time, at the store, someone threw an apple from the crate on the porch. A woman who had read something in the paper and took against what she saw. Always women. The temptation to make her displeasure physically known was too great. The first apple hit a can of macaroni on a shelf above my shoulder. The second one was caught in your hand. Ben has the athleticism and the reflexes, but I wonder about his urge to protect; how vital it is. Would he be liable to duck, or act as you did, as quick as a shot, opening your palm in front of my face to protect me from the missile? A gush of air passed through your fingers as they grabbed the apple, creating a sucking, vacuous sound. Your body was hungry for trouble. Your nervous system bristled with it. If it had been a man, you would have chased them down the street and given them a hiding, for the force of the throw was malicious, anything but child's play. But no man in town would do such a thing, for they had too much respect for you. They respected me too, in a muted, unknowing way. They respected where and with whom you lived, knowing you were too wise to shack up with a fool. That whatever went on in that house must have had a purpose because you would not be there otherwise. Your gift was too great. It was the women of the town, some of them, who had their own ideas and resentments; who felt the weight of our property rest heavily on their mind, though we were far out of their eyeline and off the beaten track. The nudity in the pictures bothered them greatly, and this was the line of argument they pursued with their husbands and others. But if pressed, those points would have crumbled because they had some memory of the beauty of their younger bodies. What they objected to was, to their perception, a life lived by whim and without any of the traditional responsibilities. On those rare times when our paths crossed, they did not seem to notice that I was as tired as they were, how my hair was similarly streaked with gray; the algebraic lines that underscored each eye. They did not hear how I stumbled over my words at the counter, only that the grocery box being filled held next to nothing beyond stationery, rice and two small bottles of liquor. The freedom held in those bottles of Kentucky rye started an acrid burning in their chests. Their faces choked on it. The countenance of the woman who threw the apple held a similar sourness. She was a cousin of Orla's sister-in-law, whose husband Edwin was a farmer up the hill. We were not strangers. Still, an object hurled with impact toward my head was more preferable to her than voicing her disgust. In their yard, stones were thrown at foxes and raccoons who scratched at the grain sacks. I too was vermin and so given the same treatment. The air between us was loaded with silent recrimination. I remember the thickness of her breath as her lower lungs wheezed into action with the exertion of the throw. She was getting older, the last of her children now helping their father on the farm in a role that was once hers. Everything she had went into the throw. With its impact nullified by a catch she had foreseen, she had nothing left. She looked to Orla across the street to pass comment. Her face was barren of feeling, deflated that the missile had not reached its target, but there was relish in her tone as she spoke. The same words she speaks now as a bundle of letters is pulled from the strongbox and handed to Ben.

– Thems above being criticized can ask for no help from the Lord when their time comes. Stands to reason. They have too many sins in their mind.

THERE ARE NO LETTERS to speak of. One packet after another fills that space behind the post office desk, but not one has come from your hand. Ben's confidence is shaken a little each time he returns from the store. Spots momentarily cloud the brightness in his eyes, until he remembers himself and works to control it. This is how families with money are raised: to put on a show. Even with me he feels the need to pretend that everything is as planned. You are out in the world having a wild time and will mail a postcard when you are ready. He knows husbands who have sailed halfway across the world before remembering to settle their wives' wits. Men who have come to their senses while their legs are wrapped around a Corsican girl; something in her mannerisms restoring the lost image of an abandoned wife. Ben is on familiar territory once the story takes hold. His uncertainty vanquished, he returns to the dealer's gentle swagger as he waves his fork at the breakfast table.

– Of course we know that isn't what's happening with him. He's not the type to do those sorts of things. His impulses lie somewhere different. He's not just going to be with somebody. He'll be out looking at a blade of grass somewhere, or riding the plains as a cowboy. You see, there's something about the weather that may be to blame, Anna. The clouds shifting in an unfamiliar pattern wherever he is; a lack of strong sunlight or rain.

– So we're waiting for clouds?

– We're waiting for clouds. Or winds. He'll be following the trail of several natural disasters, abseiling into the center of volcanoes in Hawaii. That's the kind of thing I see him doing.

The angle of his fork droops before being hastily left on the plate. He has been thinking out loud; had his thoughts catch up with him. He has never before entertained the possibility of you being in company with someone else for a prolonged period of time. He had never thought of you being worried about and cared for elsewhere. This image of you is one that we have cultivated. You are not a solitary person, not always. It has simply suited our ends to see you this way. When I think of how you are when you work on the farm, the way you greet people along the road or in the store, it is not the reticent behavior of a loner. So why would you be on your own now? Even if you have not actively sought company, you will still have it. They gravitate toward you, those who wish to be loved.

We fall silent, needing to be lost in the food. Imagining syrup to swamp our jealousy; that a bowl filled to the brim with porridge oats can hide all that we fear. It is difficult not to be wary of the other's thoughts. Each of us is unable to predict who will unearth and articulate the worst fear: that you have consciously settled down with someone else in a place not dissimilar to here; that you are not coming back. I have yet to tell Ben about your visit to St Peter's. I am not secretive by nature, but something in me holds this back. Ben keeps secrets from me, why shouldn't I do the same? Only, the preoccupation it fosters becomes a burden. Mulling over secrets hinders the work. It is why I paint what I see, what can be drawn out. Secrets are for people like Ben, loveable people whose currency is endless words, gossip. One secret revealed while a fresher one is held. He sits at the table, upright and unmoving as a mother hen, incubating secrets.

YOUR FACE IS THE FIRST to be whitewashed from the canvas; then Ben's. Less of a wash, more a series of aggressive dabs, wanting to score the canvas with my wide plasterer's brush as it pushes back and forth. For all my pounding, its shape still holds. It always amazes me how the stretched skin seems to absorb my aggression. Once I set his pose to how I want it – tighter, less exaggerated, and closer to yours – layers of paint can be built up until I will be the only one aware of your outline beneath. That you haunt the painting from the very fibers of the canvas through to the finished pose is what drives me to pick up the brush. I stare for a long time at Ben's face, knowing that it will be diminished from the weight of his mimicked pose. That although it will be the truest representation of Ben, all anyone will talk about is you. But this is still weeks away; months. For now, I wish to eradicate everything. The air in the studio is close, grown thicker like the paint. It's only outside of here that I'm conscious of having trouble breathing; the weight that sits on my chest as I lie awake in the dark. Shallowness is all that I am capable of, lapping for air the way a dog attacks a bowl of water, only here where I'm not marooned it feels easier to do so. The draft from the open door rushes across my legs and feet; a sliver of freshness from the crack in the skylight cools my forehead and the tops of my ears.

I instruct Vishni to put the box in the cellar – the crate that holds the oxygen tank and the trolley, its paraphernalia of oppression and addiction. Her eyes make a judgment all of their own, but she does as I ask. Going down there later, I see that the box has been sealed and covered with newspaper and plastic sheeting, the closest I could get to the thing being buried. They said it would make things easier, and I believed it at first, the novelty of taste and sensation telling me so, but now I know that not to be true. All relief is temporary; to look forward to that relief, to beg and watch the clock for it, subtracts a crucial element from my thinking. I've shied away from crutches throughout my life, believing that the body must survive purely through its will. The cylinder might take the pressure away from the lungs, but it would only reassert itself elsewhere, impeding my work. No one seems to understand that; it's everything that happens in this room which must take priority. I cannot paint with that thing over my mouth. If it hurts to breathe, from the closeness of the air with the omniscient fug of the oils wrapped within it, I have the kitchen to escape to, or the meadow. If life is slower, the function of my organs taxed by the effort of standing at the easel for however many hours each day, then so be it. This is what I need to do.

Pea shoots in the kitchen garden grow high as the windowsills. Their tips rustle and speak as you lift the blinds; movements intended to lure me outside. There are days when I answer the call, gathering these and zucchini flowers for use in the studio. Props to distract your wandering eyes, which roam impatiently around the debris in the studio and finally onto me; that mixture of curiosity and hunger you have, that latent energy which governs everything. The vegetation pleases you. You wave it around the easel and the upturned chair where you have been meticulously

placed. We inhale the sweetness of the leaves. Their freshness momentarily dominates the staleness of the room, the
age of the materials around us, the natural stink of our
bodies, working as we have with scant breaks for the past
few days.

– You've forgotten that the outside exists. I can see it in
your eyes. This is a reminder.

You know that freedom is imminent, have recognized
that my tiredness allows you this detour into the garden;
that sooner or later, I will perch on the couch and succumb,
sleep my exhaustion away.

Time passes differently in your head. At the moment of
release you are back outdoors with no memory of what has
gone on before. Your face draws none of it. A series of
muscle stretches are the only sign. Your concentration is
elsewhere, with Vishni or the garden. Laying on your back
and drinking beer in the long grass, goddamn hickory banjo
music blaring from the record player, studying the forma-
tion of the blades without seeming to study them at all. No
fret in your eyes. No pain or lack of comprehension at what
you see (where my faults lie). On some days what I have
asked you to do appears no more taxing or significant than
taking out the trash; a fly on your shoulder needing to be
waved away. You make everything look easy.

– We've finished for the day. You can stop being angry.

– I'm not angry.

– You are. Or you were. I thought I was going to be
murdered every time I moved. I felt the heat coming from
your face.

– Sit still then, if you want to avoid the heat.

– I didn't mind so much. It was getting chilly. The draft
was tickling my feet.

You snap me out of it with a laugh. The entire house
lifts when you are in the mood to make it so. Only when

you turn your back do I return to a half state, the weight of the unfinished painting always present in my mind until it is finished, however many months it will be.

– Where are you disappearing to? Get back here and taste these peas.

– Look at you, attacking the plant like a locust. Vishni will need them for dinner.

– There's plenty. These shoots keep growing, that's the point of it. If you're not going to lie down, stoop at least. You need to taste them straight from the plant.

– I'm familiar with peas.

– Not how they are here, right now, in this air, from this soil.

The freshness we smelled in the studio was tainted with something, the fug from the oils, my disappointment with your concentration. It sucked the brightness from the leaves and made the firm pods become limp under my touch. Didn't you notice how they didn't stay cool for long, how they wilted almost immediately? Killed by the warmth of your hand.

– Tug the pod from this stalk here, the one that's thicker than a sausage. Bite into it. Tastes alive, doesn't it? As if last night's rainwater is plumping up its fibers. How do you think that the perfume from the flowers at the top of each stalk, which Vishni has neglected to prune, has worked its way into each pea? It's sweet and crunchy and perfumed; everything I feel about the meadow as I walk through it. Don't you feel the same?

– All I can taste is . . . raw. These need to be cooked and have some butter and salt cut into them. That's the ambrosia you're looking for.

– You still surprise me. All that sight but no sense of taste. There's so much that you don't notice. As if someone took with one hand and gave with another.

You're rarely critical of me, but this is one of those times. Normally you leave all that to Ben and the women in the village. You allow Vishni her gossip when she is disgruntled. The studio is too far away to hear the words, but the tone is clear and unvarnished in its dissatisfaction. Her criticism is seldom, because she is not the kind to keep her feelings hidden, though such moments have occurred.

What are you disappointed by? That I won't bend down so that my mouth is level with yours, or that my head keeps turning back toward the house, because what sits on the easel continues to draw me back, even though my eyes sting and the muscles across my shoulders and upper arms have twisted into knots? You read too much into my face, too many things that are true: that it is better to stay inside the house because I cannot compete with your knowledge of what is outside it, farm child or no; that I am ignorant to taste, eating whatever is set before me; how I think of food as fuel rather than as a wonder.

Previously, those three or four occasions where you chided me, it was for a lack of manners or showing unkindness to someone who did not deserve it; my temper getting the better of me. When Ben, Vishni and others would lose their patience with my stubbornness, you did not encourage them; rather the opposite. You believed that, however I chose to do things – show my paintings, appear in public – was the best way for me, and loyally conveyed that to others.

One of the few things you told me: as a child you went to bed hungry when work on the docks slowed down and your father took whatever employment he could find, on one unlicensed building site after another. These weren't prolonged periods, but frequent enough during your youth; deep enough that the memory of hunger pangs stayed with you. The quiver you would feel in your gut from time to time would reconnect to a pain you thought long-since vanished. An aura you had when the table was empty, or on mornings before Vishni went to the store.

It explained why you would help birth a foal in return for a glut of apples or all the melons you could carry from ten yards of vine. Why you broke your back and the requirements of my work to build the garden beds for Vishni, when your voice, and intent, finally became as heated as mine.

You ARE FILLED WITH the stench of the city. It seeps into your skin and clothes, feeding you the way the sunlight does out here. Previously grown from fallowed soil, damp and moss now revive. You're stiff from your night in the park, but energized. Traffic noise is distant but inescapably there; children's voices as they walk to school; streams of joggers patter a well-worn path through the trees. A horse runs past you, slick and sweaty, followed moments later by her owner. All this gives you life. If you were in the meadow, you too would run, blood pumping through your body, cold air flushing the sleep from your head. You think about chasing the animal, partly because of its distress and also for the lightness you yearn for, which only comes from the speed of your legs moving over terrain. Years as a farm hand of sorts has taught you how to rein in and calm those that are frightened; how it all comes from a harmony of quick thinking and the softness of hand and voice. I have seen you sprint over the stream and across fields after a spooked foal, or cows too unsettled to join their herd. Knowledge and speed are second nature to you; your gentleness is innate. It's why you are so loved.

But you are no match for even the sluggish pace of the ill-dressed rider errantly chasing his lost status symbol. You have not run like this for some time. Your lungs can take the strain but your legs would not thank you. Walking, the persistence of walking, as you do now, is all you're capable of. Your freedom comes from the ongoing discipline of a steady pace, not breaking into a swifter movement that may impair you later, seriously or otherwise. It's a new form of fitness that has had to be explained to you now that more strenuous options have been forcibly curtailed. (It has crossed my mind that this is why you're doing this: walking to New York being the driest two-fingered salute you can think of for well-meaning doctors.) Only the horse weighs on your mind. There is an absence of riders and you worry that there is no one else nearby able to pacify her. How the wrong touch or call will send her into a more frantic mode. You've already gathered your things without realizing that you have done so. Now your feet follow the dismounted rider, who pants over a pathway fountain before the rise of a modest hill and a dense copse of elms and cedar. Your ears filter all that rushes past until you identify the sounds of hooves pounding the dirt trail, flattening the untended grass. This symmetry of panic, the one-two clop of hooves, slowing now, is the beacon you aim for. Something in that sound prompts you into more direct action, walking at pace until you have overtaken the rider, and then running through the trees.

You trample across grass in the wake of the horse. A trail of wet shit marks her nervousness. That the greater proportion of it makes contact with your shoes is of no importance. Both the docks and farms have schooled you. There is little that makes you squeamish. Shit will not make you reconsider your actions. You have been trained to run. Your memory does not let you down; your legs remember. You don't think of knee cartilages ground down until they are as flat as bone, nor the weakness in your back; only about the events that have led to her scare; whether it was the slightest miscommunication between animal and rider – a kick or jolt from the latter's leg where there was not intended to be – the malicious clap of a passer-by, or something more unexplained: that it is in the creature's nature to be skittish.

You will later say, hand on heart, that you were in no way pushing yourself, but a cursory glance behind as you make headway into the copse shows the rider still at the base of the hill, moving in a jagged, aggravated fashion. How you have overtaken him, cutting away from the hill path and through the trees, is something you will marvel over after the event, sitting in a bath of cold water at the 105th Street YMCA. For now, you press forward along the trail of shit and crushed bracken, several hundred yards of darkness until she is in sight. She is standing before a wall of trees, regal ashes that mark the heart of the park before it was created. Still yards away, you take stock of the perspiration falling in slicks off her coat and the heaviness of her breathing. You are both exhausted by the chase, something she acknowledges in the incline of her head as your hand slips through the reins. What does she read in your steps as you approach that keeps her there? What is the rhythm of your pulse as your palm strokes her face that soothes her so? The rider will tell how you were able to change the atmosphere within three steps. How a dance of 1-2-3 brought the mare to heel.

The sun remains low, barely touching the dampness of the ground and the dew held together by invisible string across foliage, yet still you remove your coat and sweater, draping them over the mare. You should not be cold. You know this, but do it anyway. Selfless, stubborn. You wipe her down with the shirt from your bag, and then you cover her, your hands moving in swift rubbing motions across and over her trunk. You are also soaked through with effort, but there is no one to pay you the same care. Your heart rates decrease, but one recovers more quickly than the other. The rider will tell me of the quiet satisfaction in your face as you continue to comfort the animal, but how this does not mask the deep tiredness that seems to radiate from every part of you.

Your pocketbook slips from your bag under the trees as you tend to the horse, its presence unnoticed until your departure. Two days later, it's returned by the rider in the mail, with five hundred-dollar bills enclosed.

All good deeds should be rewarded. You've done nothing for my pride, but you've saved me a few dollars in catching that bastard horse.

Vishni recognizes the rider's name, rifles through a stack of yellowing newspapers in the kitchen until she finds a picture. He manufactures shoes upstate and has recently completed a successful takeover of a clothing retailer in Manhattan. Despite the glow in his eyes, his lips remain in a defiantly sulky grip. This is a man who has everything to celebrate but still looks as though he wants to take on the world, person by person. Dissatisfaction glows around him, marking the pallor of his skin and setting his face into a gargoyle's rictus.

– Look at him. A scoundrel. Where is John going, to mix with men like him?

In a second letter, responding to the enquiries to the incident, he wrote:

He was beat in a way that had little to do with the horse, that's what I thought. He had the eyes of someone doing his damndest to run himself into the ground. It was only something I thought about afterwards, that he'd pushed himself almost past the point of what his body could support. And he looked like nothing, this guy. His teeth were good, the shirt, but everything else . . . you can understand why I thought he might rob, or ask for money, at least.

I swung for him before I spoke, I remember that. I didn't touch him. My fist was nowhere near him, but the frustration of getting up that damn hill, and finding him standing there so placidly with her, as if I was the one at fault, made me lash out. The horse kicked up a bit, but his hand was still on the reins and he had her calmed in the time it took me to pull back my punch. He has an even tone of voice, your guy. 'I was worried when I saw her get away from you,' he said. 'Something must have frightened her. She's had a time of it, but she'll be fine now.'

Truth is, his gentleness was making things worse. There was words I wanted to call him. Shameful things that belied the good turn he had done, which I kept to myself, because even I understood that shouting before the horse would only spook her again and start the chase anew. My heart couldn't take any more damn running.

It was then that he looked as if he was in some pain from the run. I couldn't look at him. Didn't want him anywhere near me. I held out fifty dollars, but he wouldn't take it. I'm a man of the world. I know how money makes every difficult passage smoother, but he looked at me like I was the one with shit on my hands, not him. All that came from him was a very intent stare, as if he had moved his attention from her and was now attempting to calm me. You can't swear a blue streak in that atmosphere. It's unholy. And like I said, I didn't want to rile up the horse. It was easier to take the reins and send him away.

I saw what you saw: how hatefully he must have stared at you when he finally reached you and the horse. The insults he'd taken pains to keep from me; how easily they would have tumbled from his mouth. How it was only the

78

muck on your hands from when you had slipped (where? How badly?) that held him back from brushing you with his fists. That the money was not offered, but thrown into the mud and shit, as if that was where you came from and still deserved to be. Even once he was aware of your name he did not wish to encounter you in the park again. Reminders of his ineptitude were avoided. Similarly, the horse was sent to another stable on the other side of the park where he would not have to see her again. He didn't regret his actions.

EVEN WITHOUT YOUR POCKETBOOK, you can't bring yourself to check in at our hotel. With your last fifty dollars, you find a bed at the Y and bathe away the puffiness from your legs and knees. A series of cold tubs to somehow trick the body out of its stiffness, a remedy they use on the farms after plowing and harvest. In a lower bunk, where you rest for the next two days, it is tenderness that you feel the most; how sore the skin on your body feels, painful to the fingertips. Discoloration from the bruising on your shins and kneecaps where you fell, losing your footing on the uneven track as you left the park.

You lie on your back, spread-eagled and prone, the only position you can sustain without any sound coming from your mouth.

There is attention at the Y if you want it. Age does not always divide here, as it does in other parts of the city. The four-bunk room you share is not without its fellows: men in their twenties and thirties visiting the city for the first time; two busboys at Studio 54 in the room across the hall. There is something of home in your face that they all respond to. You are not snobbish about some of their clunky ways; nor their ruddy, well-fed faces, or too-smart shoes. That open, plain friendliness is not something to be looked down upon, as it is in most of the bars downtown. The boys bring you painkillers, coffee and food. Directions are sought, also advice on better jobs, and leisure, and where best to make a home so that both of these things can be achieved. Wounds from their home towns are covered over with hopefulness. They talk very little about those places, reducing them to a postmark fading into a smudge. At night, when they are back from the bars, rejected and disheartened, you hear them seek comfort as one relieves another.

When you feel strong enough to stand, you make your way downstairs, walking on the balls of your feet, like a child, to avoid putting adverse pressure on your joints. You call St John at the bank and make arrangements. You accept now that a financial cushion is needed, that keeping your strength and health is not an indulgence but something that should remain pertinent in your mind. St John accommodates, as per your instructions, each murmur reminding that he is there to serve. Knowing us as he has done for these many years, however, he is aware of the weariness in your voice; even without seeing you, he recognizes that some vital spark has been lost in the months since the two of you last met. He makes gentle overtures about calling Ben to arrange a transfer to the hotel we normally favor, how he is happy to do it if you do not wish Ben to be informed. The nature of your call, your tiredness, suggests secrecy, and he wants to spare you embarrassment. Nevertheless, the mention of the Y strains the credulity in his voice. He understands your need for independence from me, how that has always been so, but clearly he is shocked. There must be more comfortable places you could be staying. Anonymity, if that is what you require, need not cost that high a price. Another time, you would brush his concerns away, confident in your decision. If you could slip from this unrelenting grip of exhaustion, you'd hang up and hail the first cab to collect your money. Instead you pack your things and wait for him in the hall. You take a last fill of the noise and scent from the Y: the slamming of doors, shouts and yells of fraternal love, the depth of musk and muscle, top notes of cheap aftershave and marijuana, before allowing St John to help you into the car.

St John has the foresight not to entrust a cab driver with so delicate a journey, instead choosing to drive himself. You are squeezed into the modest cabin space of his town car, suppressing the desire to shout when your legs compress to fit the foot well. Though you sit in traffic for the next half-hour as St John navigates the park toward his apartment on the Upper West Side, he has the good sense not to speak. The journey is one of reflection for you both. At several points – driving through the park, at West 74th and 6th – you consider asking him to turn around; not for the Y, but to drop you at Penn Station. The spaciousness of a Pullman car, and a stiff drink. You think of your room in the house and the welcoming partial darkness there. You think of Vishni's careful ministrations and the space that I will give you; that there'll be no questions. It would be so easy to return and fall back into the shade of our home; except, your list is far from being completed. There is still too much you have to see. In a guestroom heavy with crushed velvet and lavender, you convalesce for a further day. St John's housekeeper lacks Vishni's attention to detail, but there is tea, soup, bread and, later, a tender poached chicken and dumplings. Stronger now, you attack the plate with relish and ask for more. You allow the presence of a doctor, but only briefly, long enough to confirm that you are of sound health to continue; short enough to avoid his sermon. The verdict is that ultimately your suffering has not been so serious as to hamper your undertaking. You'll live.

You stay wrapped deep within the frills of your room. St John is not a man given to opulence, but there is richness to the furnishings throughout the apartment that gives you butterflies. There are paintings, though this is not the source of your unease. Paintings are a point of familiarity; you know the chaos of their origins and do not equate them, specifically the money that is sometimes paid for them, with something obscene. It is more the thickness of the carpets and the gilt-edging that outlines furniture and glassware that triggers your nausea. The apartment is simple and at the same time not so. You have dined at more luxurious houses, yet something about knowing how St John has founded his wealth – from the same visual agony he displays on his walls – makes your stay an unsettling one. You know where you stand with industrialists and politicians. The viscous nature of money as a business, a banker trading off and on the money made from your image on canvas is less opaque. You are gracious for his hospitality, but feel as though you are walking on eggshells. He studies you with the inquisitiveness of a benefactor: how well you sleep and the amount you eat. From time to time his eyes stray to the phone on your bedside table; how hard he is fighting the impulse to telephone me.

St John knows the work, its range and development over the years. He comes to the few shows that have taken place in New York and goes out of his way to see others during his holidays. He will take a train to Valencia following a conference in Madrid; ask his driver to stop at the National Portrait Gallery en route to the Bank of England. He knows every contour of your face; knows what is happy and what is otherwise. The doctor's visit has reassured him; now he worries less about your physical state, only that which he can't see. It's not blankness as such, more a reticence to discuss why you are here and where you are going. No explanation has been offered for why you were sleeping in the park. He is a man who speaks little, so when he sits on your bed for those twenty minutes during his lunch hour, it is a conversation of silence, space and presence. Still you offer nothing.

Only when you are on the train – wrapped up in one of his cashmere sweaters, a basket of provisions carefully packed into your laundered duffel bag – do you reflect on your stay. House guests, whatever the state of their health, need to reflect back the generosity of their hosts. There was no glimmer when St John studied you, only dullness; a patent lack of manners which you now regret, away from the stifling atmosphere of the house. In the same way that I have taken on some of your words – the 'Goddamn Almighty!' you picked up from a Saturday-morning Western as a boy and never let go of – you have unknowingly absorbed the tenets of my selfishness. When you are with me it's a despised behavior that we argue over; away from me it flourishes. I have known you to stand up and leave the table once you have finished eating, regardless of your hosts. Your impatience at the vanities of some art curators and collectors is no longer concealed in their company; farmed eccentricities are something to be despised. St John sees what I see: a man falling back into what he has been taught, that everything should be said without words. Expression is to blame. The faces you have learned.

The concession begins in the journey to the station. In the traffic, you thaw. Your paranoia that St John is updating Ben or myself – whether he has or not – ceases to be important. The warmth of the car reminds you of where you were found, in the draftiness of the Y. How spartan it was. You recognize that thanks must be given, even at this late juncture. St John intuitively knows what is happening but does not accelerate anything. His neck is flushed with expectation but he quietly breathes it away. That is the mark of the man who has rescued you; of the respect he holds you in. You have no idea of how you are seen, do you? Even now. Of the talent you have.

– I hope that you'll pardon me if you have found anything wanting in my manners. I have guests so rarely I'm never entirely sure what is expected of me.

His turn of speech moves with the traffic, slow and hesitant, as if these are neither the right words nor direction, but something nevertheless that he has committed to. All that spares your embarrassment is the absence of direct contact, the pair of you keeping your eyes on the road.

– In the bank, nothing is beyond my capabilities. There are surprises and pressures that can push me to my limit – that's what being responsible for money does: stretches you to breaking point – but I am never at a loss. A customer we've had for many years, who's now losing his mind, comes in and demands we open an account for his dog. I call our printer and arrange for a checkbook to be made with a box for a paw print instead of a signature. This is my role. Anything outside my realm I amass and learn. It is only at home that I can be uncertain. I guessed from your condition that it was quiet that you needed most. When I found you in that place, you looked like a ghost. Tell me if I did right, bringing you here. I need clarification in this area.

Of this you are capable.

– It's all to do with the hands. They teach you this in school. Strong posture is necessary for people to have confidence in you. You're the flagpole that they flutter against. Chest out and shoulders back; feet spread a sensible width apart. Not one leg hooked over another like a Broadway dancer. And the hands: firmly, but not rigidly locked behind your back. It means that you give your full attention to whoever's speaking with your entire body. In employing any other posture I have a tendency to daydream. I feel looser. Not as alert or capable. Is it an issue of standards? That is what I'm thinking has brought you to New York. Is it the filth you wanted to see? The greed? In which case, it's not the YMCA you need, but the dining room at the Plaza, or the basement offices at some of the museums your woman has dealt with. Away from artists and executors, these people hide nothing; their faces are filled with the hunger of acquisition and ownership. This is how they breathe. Anything you want to tell me will stay between us. It's always been that way, even if your body language believes otherwise. I take my friendships as seriously as I do my other responsibilities. If money is what this city chooses to worship, then think of me as your priest. If family can emerge not from blood but loyalty and attention paid over decades, then think of me as your brother. Whatever you say won't leave this car.

There was an afternoon more than ten years ago when you were alone together and he was similarly insistent. Drunk on your summer blondness; how sunshine had created something that incandescent. Something feral in his glance to suggest he was close to grabbing your arm; forgetting the much-boasted posture to plead. With carnality rejected, the pursuit of knowledge, your mind, is all he has to reach for. It never strays far from your thoughts that he is a financier by profession. One who hunts opportunities the way you track game in the fields. You will not be encircled like a deer or rabbit intended for table. You are all too aware of those tricks. But his kindness stops you from being hard. You have fallen back on this all your life. You wouldn't have stayed with me otherwise.

– The doctor says things, and his words hang in the air. Feels as if we're offered an unwanted gift. Something we'd rather not touch or acknowledge. Except, it comes for her, whether or not she wants it.

– There are second opinions. Other avenues. Doctors

can be changed if their manner is too brusque, although I always thought that plainness of speech would be something she'd appreciate.

– She's dying. Something that I can't mention or acknowledge in her presence. It's easier to take myself away. Easier for her. She shouldn't be distracted by my face and what it betrays.

– Even without looking at you, your worry swamps the car. It must've been tough in the house. Knowing your body can betray you, the way hers is betraying her.

– In the time that's left, I'm seeing all there is to see. I want to study things, paintings, the way people study me. It's a curiosity I have.

Your hands rest firmly on his shoulder. A fraternal gesture; momentary but wanted. It's as much reassurance as you can give to a worried mind.

THERE IS NOW FORM to Ben's body but little in the face. What I see there seems to change at each sitting, as if he too is unsure; both of us in apprenticeship. He has settled into the routine and understands what is required of him: to sit, stretch and sit again. His life in this house is to be under my command, but still the process relies on what he willingly gives. Neither of you fought in the war. Ben was stationed in Arkansas and never posted; your ineligibility for combat. It makes me wonder whether this element was missing in your life: the marking of time as a foot soldier, whether in the army or not; the ability to be a drone and follow orders without thinking. Except, in the absolute stillness of the moment, standing in front of me in the studio, the submissive argument crumbles. There is only enough energy to concentrate on being who you are. For all the staginess in coercing your body into the shape that will best work, nothing is artificial. Nowhere to hide.

Ben's interest grows. After mealtimes, in the hour during which Vishni forces me to rest, he returns to the studio and studies the canvas. Aside from the progress made, he notes its height and depth, wondering as much about the possible home for it, as what it will eventually capture of him. His mind races, making up for the time lost when he sits before me, blank as a cipher. The phone calls he makes in his room after dinner relate only to the work. He describes in detail the physical progress of the day; the scores that have marked the canvas; how much color spent. He pauses after every note, sometimes at length, suggesting the effort of an assistant on the other end of the line, accurately recording his words. What purpose does this record hold? Where will they go? Ben has seen paintings in progress before – no different to thousands of eggs on a battery farm waiting to hatch – but never has he been so forensic in what he observes. His sharpness, that which Vishni and myself over-hear from the corridor, is refreshing. But we are also wary. What else does he notice?

On his instruction, the gallery sends a lithograph of the painting, the one that's in our minds. We never speak of it, recognizing a mutual understanding of why Ben is posed the way he is; why he still wears your striped sweater for his time in the studio. There are others who think there are better paintings: the one of you with the farm dogs that made the front of the *New York Times*; another of Vishni sitting on the same sofa where Ben now sits. 'There,' they will say. 'These are the definitive works. These are the portraits that made her name. What we will remember her by.' Almost all the paintings they think of feature you, although not in this jumper or pose. Maybe it's forgotten because it was bought so quickly at its first show, or possibly because that particular show featured predominantly nudes; its naturalness lost in the stampede for flesh. There are no favorites in painting, only those that you think about, learn from, are haunted by. This is one of those.

We are not meant to know about the lithograph. It is hidden at the bottom of the chest of drawers in your room (where Vishni discovered it). Every night we hear him pull it from its cardboard sleeve and unwrap the tissue that protects it. Sometimes he does this while he is talking on the phone. It appears that the person on the other end of the line also has a copy, and in these sessions they compare various details: the degree to which a head is tilted; how the leg was raised to give that degree of definition without stretching the calves to breaking. It is one of the older assistants that Ben trusts. One of the women who live and breathe the business; understanding the extent of his capabilities. He wouldn't be so collaborative otherwise; bouts of silence in the room as he listens to counter arguments to whatever he suggests. In the studio, Ben remains as insular as he needs to be; outside, he makes clear his need to document it, requiring his assistant to conspire, bear witness. His bookshelves in the Provincetown house are lined with biographies and diaries belonging to artists and their muses. Is it his experience being recorded, or mine?

Vishni would cry after her early sittings. Tears falling into her soup. The cumulative effect of posing over an extended period of time is intensive and draining. Everything you have to give has been squeezed out. Everything you wanted to hide will come to the fore. I study the walk of those sitters as they leave the studio; a previously sturdy gait broken down into something softer; defeated. A funereal shuffle to the nearest bed. The stagger of an exhausted workman who has expended all he has during his shift. You were always tired. It was natural for you to be that way. But you were never truly empty. You slept, it's true. Stayed quiet as you ate your food. But there was still something in reserve; a look in your eye that suggested you were far from being worn. It came from the same store of determination that made you half-cross the country, bringing you to me. Ben's account – whatever he is doing – is an attempt to build his own reserves. By observing as much as he can, taking in every detail the way I do with him, he creates a parallel picture; one that may be preferred.

– The eye is there. The pace is there. It's unbelievable

what she's doing. That she would think of doing this. The energy she has when she's in the room. The concentration. You could heat a stove for a month with the energy that comes from it. No. She looks unwell. Shockingly so, since I last saw her. There's strength there. She's still moving the canvases around and won't accept any help with them. Something in that room brings her to life; the work itself; the need to complete it. When we're away from there, though . . . I look at her in the kitchen sometimes and I . . . It's been three years since I last saw her. How does the body do that in three years? She knows, I think, but doesn't acknowledge it. All that matters to her is getting it right. This.

You're revived; the speed of the train under your feet doing its work, but also pulsing from the bag you hold to your chest, packed with the bills counted with care by St John. 'Money makes everything fizz,' you once said disparagingly, as we sat in a Manhattan auction house and watched the work of a Master be reduced to goods in a fire sale; painting after painting streaming by, as if they were nothing more than pallets of white goods to be cleared.

– Look at them waving their paddles. Congratulating each other on how civilized their greed is. They might as well be blowing bubbles, for all the care they take in throwing their money around.

You despise yourself for the amount of cash you hold and the ease with which it was given. It partly explains the barrier that holds back any real honesty with St John. For all his helpfulness and loyalty, he remains our enabler. A reminder of where this money has come from, how it was earned.

The train carries you out of the city and past the garden states, turning southwest toward the plains and wilds you never thought you would see. Excluding our house and the farms, the city is all you've ever known: the place of your birth, and those cities I have taken you to where what we do is in demand. The accepted knowledge is that the dustbowl towns with their homeliness and limited horizons hold nothing for us; that the reticence shown by some of our neighbors to the paintings and the way we live is heightened, where intolerance becomes decisive action. That if we set up shop in any of these one-horse places, we'd be run or burnt out of town. Alone, the outcome differs. You can roam and blend. One small town after another will fall to your charms, your ease with strangers, the fact that you are naturally friendly and not suspicious the way I am. You will leave your mark on those places, if that is what you wish. The creek that runs between our house and the trio of farms that border the meadow now carries your name, a sign of the affection you are held in. What is there to stop this from happening elsewhere?

If this comes to mind, it does not do so until you have seen what you needed to see in Kentucky and are back on a vehicle rolling well beyond the state line. From the moment you set foot on Kentucky asphalt, you are only concerned with finding your bearings and reaching your destination. It is one of the larger towns: one that can soak up the pangs of the city for those who can only measure life in bricks and mortar, restaurants, cabs. The tea parlor off Main Street with its lace curtains covering the lower half of the windows suggests an owner who may have read about – or visited – the Russian Tea Room in New York. The three-story department store brings all the fashions and modernizations from the outside world. You can have your sophistication legitimized via the Art, Literature and Poetry Society; your otherness confirmed by the dances between men that take place in the hardware store basement every quarter month. Despite the clement weather, a woman hurries from her car in a short fur of a dull, muddy luster. Only the patent leather of her shoes reflects in the storefront glass as she crosses the road. A tractor heading out of town slows to allow her safe passage. There is something that makes you feel at home: the familiar and rarefied (although your clothes would not pass muster in the department store; similarly at the diner, where your duffel bag and coat are indentified as a hobo uniform, until the waitress sees your shoes and the camera strap hanging around your neck).

The museum is built on a corner plot, a block west from the farthest end of Main Street, where the road reduces to a trail in both directions, as if to span what is the true heart of the town. An imposing Italianate building that as recently as twenty years ago was more congruous to its neighbors as a residential home. Only the wrought-iron railing, almost as tall as the eves, and the stone steps leading from the wide front door to the bricked path give the building its civic air. Not grand as such, but intended to demonstrate something greater than homespun, in the same way that a school or church sets itself apart from its neighbors to signify that value and respect must be placed here (and if that is not possible, fear). The museum and what it stands for has joined this trinity. You expect to have the building to yourself. Your impatient pull of the door, the fast walk along the hallways and into the first of a series of linked rooms that houses the small collection, suggest this. The next train is six hours away. You have not traveled this far to rush, but that first sight, the one you have in your mind's eye from the moment you left St John, weighs heavily. It pumps blood around your body and leaves your head swimming with sweet anticipation. The rooms themselves are sparsely furnished, arranged in no particular theme or logic, bar the taste of its curator. For all the space afforded by lack of tables and benches, the first cases are intensely packed with miniature terra-cotta sculpture and cameos; China and Regency England sitting in close proximity. The low positions of the spot lamps ensure that you walk in partial gloom, making the house seem much older than it is. The small windows, with their meager allowance of light, count for nothing here. The intention is to enter a treasure cave, leaving the tribulations of the wheat field or textile mill behind. A noticeboard between the second and third rooms advertises a guided tour that is yet to be taken up. Its lined space to accommodate the names of interested parties is bare; the notice itself yellowing at the edges. A plaque displaying an unnamed coat of arms is nailed beside it; a wooden shield that bears the colors of a racing team you once admired. Though it is not intended as such, this is the first piece that you stand before and contemplate; thinking of home.

What triggers memory can never be clearly divined. You look at those colors and think about watching junk-car racing with your brother on Coney Island. Hot dogs slicked in your hands, shouting yourselves hoarse as you cheer your chosen car to smash the hell out of the others. You haven't thought about the track for years; the dust that got inside your shoes; the heat and noise of the men around you. The plaque imbibes the smell of petrol filling your teenage nose; the grease from the hot dog sitting in a thick film across your lips and palm. Your brother. His face. You cannot remember when you last brought him to mind, for his face is yours. It is all the reminder you need. As you continue to walk through the rooms you are aware of the taste of bacon on your breath from the diner, a further blanket of memory that sits on your shoulders; that keeps back the draft. Boiled bacon and potatoes in your mother's kitchen. Your brother and yourself eating dinner before your father returned. The nervousness you all felt. A flood of forgotten feeling coming from a badge.

You question the wisdom in what you are doing. In satisfying your curiosity you wish to pick and choose. The possibility of other long-forgotten or repressed memories coming to the fore is not a welcome one. It is not chronic unhappiness that you have known. You are not troubled by melancholy. Never have been. But I have changed you, and even if your temperament remains constant, you do not wish to be reminded so minutely of what you were before. You only wish to recognize the innate, not the accumulation of knowledge; how far you have come.

There is a bench in the second-to-last room where you sit and rest, more tired than you realized. The heaviness in your legs has returned; the muscles are tight; feet, numb. In your eagerness to get here you have lost track of the miles you have walked from the station; the blocks circled and turned back upon to find your way without help. The paintings are here; yours hanging over a defunct, tiled fireplace. Your memory of the expression you held has been hazy until you see it. You think of a photographic negative being washed in a chemical bath. How details come forth in waves: sharpness suddenly appearing, before blurring back into the red light of the dark room. Now you can recall the distant look on your face and some of the thinking behind it. You were wishing yourself out of the studio. Hating me; wishing my death. We didn't argue when this portrait was painted – something that began as a commission that eventually fell through; an office trophy for an industrial executive who decided to move on to a more fashionable artist – but you were angry with me for putting you through these movements, and with yourself for complying.

I worked on six portraits that year in order to be ready for the show. There was no time to do anything else. The house fell into disrepair for several months. Dirt spread. We ate bread and raw food, drank coffee and cold water straight from the outside tap. Both you and Vishni sitting. The three of us, a factory that burned day and night. We were all exhausted. It is not the expression you remember, but the understanding of what your life is: to sit and be painted. How nothing else could stand before or against it. There was no argument more pressing or greater obligation to be fulfilled. You were required to hold your bladder and your tongue, being yourself all the while and somehow reflecting the interests and loves that were temporarily withheld. So as you look at the painting, you discern the shimmering creek in your face, its glint both welcome and cruel in the sun shining through the window. Your forehead and cheeks were brown from working the fields in the evening; a three-hour break during which Vishni took your place. Dust from the fields settles in the deep grooves across both knees, from when you were following the plow in the neighboring field; a detail that sent me raging at first until I realized that it was there to be used. You are sitting in a chair looking away from me. Your brow is thick; your lips pursed, deep in thought. The palm of one hand grips the knuckles of the other. You are ready to spring from the chair and attack whoever is looking at you, if the look or words are not to your liking. The moment when life as you knew it changed; the understanding that what we did here was truly seen. What you did in the fields of no importance to anyone who saw this in the gallery. You are here to be studied, commented upon, and sometimes loved. This is when you understand.

Memory acts like a trigger again, so that you find your-self resuming some of the old postures. From the center of the bench you hunch your shoulders and cross your legs, pushing forward on the balls of your feet as if to spring. There is nothing relaxed about the position; the intention is to see the definition of your body pushing through clothes; a similar strain flashing across your face. Everything about the painting is the moment. You are not in the habit of photographing yourself, but for once you wish to mark the correlation. You recognize the rarity of opportunity, knowing that you will never visit this town again. You trust that you have left the exposure where it should be, as you stay perfectly still and take your pictures. Camera held at arm's distance, a surge of heat rushes through your body, as if only the popping of the flashbulb allows you to admit that this is something pleasurable. That, for all the uncertainty, you can always find solace in how you were trained. There is something comforting about pushing your body this way. Often you find yourself doing it unconsciously: the stretch of your leg into the carriage aisle as you traveled to Kentucky; the triangle formed of elbow and arm behind your head as you sat upright in bed and awaited the arrival of St John. Shucking corn from the fields at harvest time: the expansion of your hands as they threw sheaths onto the collection truck as it drove back and forth. The way that you hold your coffee cup and fork eggs from a steaming hot plate. The division between movements is blurred between what is natural and what is staged.

You place the camera on the arm of the bench and take several more pictures, both of the room and yourself. The partial darkness of the room, the space it affords, is familiar. The unrelenting cold of the floor as you lie on it is no different to being in the studio; a blank space where precision is favored over comfort. The poses you worked toward and rejected until you reached the final piece; those where you stood atop the chair and then underneath it. Cobwebs blooming from the corners of the ceiling, the shadow from the doorway cast upon the lower half of the painting. All this you record. Everything that goes through your mind.

You are unaware of how the time passes until you are gently awoken from the bench. It is almost dark and a woman stands over you.

– I was wary of disturbing you, looking so comfortable there. But it's six o'clock and I need to close the museum otherwise I shall miss my bus.

It takes you several moments to recognize the short fur coat, glossy for the most part but matted at the sleeves and hem; the woman you had seen earlier that afternoon. She is in her late forties, compact and neat like a doll, her hair, pinned back, of a similar candied luster to the coat.

– Have you been here all this time?

– For the last hour or so. I leave the place open while I run my errands. The old man who owns it doesn't seem to mind.

– Even in a town like this, that doesn't strike me as particularly safe.

Her laugh is dry, unoffended.

– There's very little here worth stealing. Detritus the old man's picked up and hoarded over the years. I'm not sure he even knows what half of it is.

– I would be inclined to take more care.

– Folks know one another in this town. Thieving's restricted to cattle and what grows in the fields, or sometimes a neighbor's wife. Nothing more.

She loathes this town. Her look is one of disdain, but as with others in whom home-soil has settled in their blood, clogging their arteries, she will fight with all comers in its defense. You think of your parents and the gloom of the muddy Hudson in their eyes; damp air sticking to their chests and the interminable scratch of rodent claws against brick as they ran between walls. They couldn't live with or without their surroundings.

– You look disorientated.

– I'm OK. Slept very deeply, is all. I find this bench comfier than a bed for some reason. Product of a Depression-era childhood.

– The old man has the same tongue. 'An honest man with nothing to hide should be able to sleep on nothing more ornate than a plank of wood.' 'A poor background shouldn't equal a poor mind' is another.

– He sounds interesting.

– On a good day. The rest of the time he's a taskmaster.

– Plantation owner with a Botticelli?

– One and the same. Why don't I make you some coffee before you go? You're still looking beat. I have an office across the hall. He says it's for staff only, but I guess he wouldn't disapprove, seeing that you shared a Depression and everything. I'm Laurel, by the way.

– John.

They are just words to her: Depression, Crash – historical anomalies that belong in this room. She speaks them as if reciting a list of foods to be avoided, the corners of her mouth tightening with every syllable.

As you sit in her office – as much a storeroom as it is administrative – you watch her shoulders drop, mouth and chin losing some of that earlier rictus. She grows more comfortable with you as the coffee brews, suggesting her testiness with men of your age isn't as set as she'd like it to appear. What starts as a hardened act of charity – she can never be entirely sure whether you are one of the old man's friends, one who neglected to mention the fact – warms into something easier: the glow of a good deed performed well. After a day of hardness, supervising an exuberant school group on a short tour who quelled their boredom by spitting on the banisters, arguing with a girl at the lunch counter over being short-changed, nagging the old man to pay a handful of bills, most of all the electricity, she is as much in need of kindness as you are.

The mouth of the desk holds two chairs, one empty, another stacked with 24-month calendars; the old man's thrift rather than hers. She has the air of someone who'd blow all the money in an instant because she's so sick of the crumbling place. Turning the building into something else, anything, and razing all the contents, everything old or connected to that much-despised word *antique*.

She perches on the edge of the desk and starts sipping her coffee before you do – prefers the scalding sensation reaching her teeth and lips rather than anything remotely tepid. Thrill, as much as impatience. She understands that you are slower; in a glance registering that you don't touch your cup until she has long since set hers down. This is the meaning of hospitality: allowing for differing ingestion regimes; knowing that she needs to employ every fiber of patience she has to wait for the drink to cool and watch you consume it. All her self-control not to shout or fill the mug with cold water, as she would do for her employer.

You want to ask whether the old man is still around. Whether he is who you think he is. Seeing the painting remains the most important thing. There is no marker to register how seeing it again has changed you, other than you now feel both older than you did but at the same time younger, as if something of the painting's essence has been imbibed. If the woman does not recognize the correlation in eyes, he is bound to. Something in the face will resonate, even if your body fails you as you sit exhausted in the chair.

– I'm guessing you don't have a hotel room or anywhere to go if you're spending the afternoon sleeping in the house of horrors.

– It's a beautiful place. There are some great things here.

– To me it holds everything but beauty. All that is dead and unwanted. Can't you smell it? The sourness of age that sticks to everything here?

– I come from that place. This is my smell.

– I wasn't being personal. I get angry with this stuff. No one has any idea what it takes to keep the place going. The money poured in to keep the leaflets printed and the lights on.

– I'm teasing you. But I understand what you mean about paintings. If they don't speak to you in some way, they may as well be dead for the value they have.

– I work for a sleep-deprived old man who's not above ringing the house at two a.m. if he has an idea that needs to be sounded out. Improving the numbers. How to present myself better. You still haven't told me where you're staying, by the way.

– I've just got here. I have no idea where I'm staying. If I'm staying at all.

– I have an image of you walking alone at night. I'm not sure where that came from.

– Your old man keeps similar habits, I'm guessing.

– He doesn't take to the street, that's for sure, but the restlessness is there. He's at the stage where he's too scared to close his eyes in case they don't open again. I guess this is what awaits most of us in old age, that we become sleeping experiments. My grandmother was the same.

– Zombies cursed to live.

– That's the spirit!

– I don't live on the streets.

– I wasn't suggesting that.

– I've lived on the streets, briefly, when I was very young. A period of hand-to-mouth when I was trying to find my way in the world. There was no money in this country for a long time. It should paralyze you, but actually it does the opposite. You're unable to sit still. Looking. Always looking.

– I won't joke about the glory days, but this isn't what you're doing now, is it? Because the road doesn't suit you. You're exhausted.

– I'm traveling for as long as I need to. Seeing all there is to see. For any peace to come, you must discover whether your life has had meaning. I heard a Holy fellow preach this once. Always stayed with me.

– The old man isn't scared of a row. There's no one he fears in this town, but he knows that I live alone most of the time. That there won't be a man who answers the ringing phone at two a.m. to give him hell. Clearly, it works both ways. I've called him a couple of times too, when I've been upset by other things. In return, this is what I have to put up with: the ghost house. Mostly free of visitors, bar the twice-weekly tours for school brats. The town, on the whole, isn't interested in what we have here.

– Except me.

– Except you. That's why I'm giving you coffee. Every act of curiosity needs its reward. If you were younger, the reward may have differed. They give out fancier prizes in other towns, I'm sure, but dime-store coffee from the ghost house is as good as any. Who knows, you might find something in the bottom of your cup, if you're lucky.

– Such as?

– A stained bottom dating back from the poor excuse for tea drunk by the Pilgrims. Cracked porcelain, because he won't let me buy cups that are better made. That's the best I got.

She stares at you now, as though she is the man in the car and you are the one walking with care along the street; hunger in her eyes for knowledge. She studies your face and hands, your clothes and bag. They fall onto your good shoes and stay there for a while. She knows.

– I don't pay attention to what the old man brings into the place. He won't come during opening hours because he doesn't like to mix with people. Can't stand their ignorance, he says, which is a funny thing to say for someone so keen on educating the town. The school visits, the buses taking the brats to and from, the lunches that they must have, the tour books with stories about some of the paintings and artifacts, of which they are all given a copy to take home. All this comes from his pocket. The schools couldn't care less one way or another about these tours or stories. They only get worked up about algebra scores and football scholarships. He had to fund building a new football field and locker room for them to get interested. He restocked the library too, but they took that for granted. Only a landscaped pitch, with shiny aluminum bleachers and a boiler tank for the heroes of the field to soap themselves down in style, would grant him respect. This is the other reason why they hate him so: for making them do what they don't want. Having to pay their regards in their lunch hour. Send their wives over with cakes the maid has baked, or the last of the good chutney they were saving for Christmas. For making his money into a whip or a gun held above their heads. He plays the tune, not the other way around. He's not beholden to the dancing mice. He comes after I've closed up, or later. Some of the late-night calls I've taken have been made here. 'I'm moving the furniture around,' he says. 'It's getting too stuffy. I'm adding some brightness' – meaning a new painting

104

to greet me in the morning, or a cracked vase that looks like it belongs in the trash. He's none too agile in his later years. In the winter, when the cold seizes his joints, he has to use a stick. There's a man in the house, Oscar, who does all the driving and repairs, so I guess that's where some of the muscle comes from. If he doesn't call in the morning when I open up, I'll find a handwritten map of the new layout and copies of the mounting cards that he's had printed and placed. Everything is thought of. All to his timetable.

It's the talk of time that makes you shift in your chair. Your train has been missed but that is not the chronology you think of. It is the calendar of tissue and bone, blood flow and organ function; of age. The old man is in control of all timetables but this one. Age will not be paid or quietened.

– I read the cards but don't pay attention to the exhibits. Not in the detail that he wants. I'm the only one who can put up with his horse-crazy rituals. If he could find another woman fool enough to deal with him, I would have been fired long ago. I memorize what he's written and recite it on the tours. It's the tone of my voice and the rhythm of my delivery. I might as well be singing a song to them for how smooth and musical it is. They walk around in a daze as if I'm singing them a lullaby. Either that or they're wondering how to spend their 25 cents in the shop. He gives them spending money too. No one looks at anything, not really, just the sound of my voice and following my footsteps. 'Anna Brown. Born 1905. American portrait painter said to show the changing heart of the country conveyed through two life models. Her work is found in collections worldwide including her only self-portrait, one of her earliest works, in the National Library in Washington. *Rug 52* depicts her model of choice, John Brown, a decade into their working relationship, and is a good example of her naturalism and tone.'

– Very good. I've no complaints.

– Is there anything you'd add? He welcomes feedback if it's constructive.

– Something more about John Brown. 'Born 1910 in New York. Lived with the artist for most of his adult life. In later years, he built a portfolio of photographs depicting a similar way of life that Anna explored in paint.'

– That I can do.

– Not so much for the model's vanity, but just some concrete details to show that he existed. That he wasn't imagined on that canvas.

– More words to memorize, is all. Put them in their right place. Means nothing to me other than that. I don't think any of the rascals I take on the tour give a hoot whether that particular painting once hung in our embassy in Toronto or a movie star's bowling alley.

– They don't ask questions?

– Yes, but no one who visits has any greater knowledge, aside from some smart-alecks who turn up once or twice a year to study that particular painting and a couple of others. I won't tell you which ones they are. You'll have to guess them.

– I do?

– Though I suppose to someone like you who must know something about this stuff it's glaringly obvious, like a prize bull standing in the midst of a group of breeding heifers.

– You only say that because you've had your fill. It's not what you believe.

– As far as this town is concerned, we're the bulls and they're the heifers: simple creatures that breed and shit, and then trample the grass.

– We're all simple creatures, when you think about it. What our needs are. I was told once that this is what good painting captures: the simplicity that is buried under all the other complications.

– I like that. You've had good teachers. Knowledge, the sharing of it, is what keeps the old man going. He thrives on the idea that somewhere there will be a kid for whom this jumble makes sense. That they'll find a painting or statue to inspire. Use those blessed cards to form a pathway out of here.

– Genius comes from unexpected places.

– Picasso came from the back streets of Spain.

– There you are.

– The poor bastard is waiting for Christ, or at least his equivalent in Art. Someone to show that his work hasn't been in vain. Or mine, for that matter.

– It can happen. It can happen anyplace. I've seen it.

– Seeing you so concentrated as you sat in front of that painting, I wondered whether it was you. Something in your face went beyond that of a spectator, even those rare ones who know something about Art. What's good and what isn't. You're in that painting somehow, aren't you? Your blood is there.

She speaks softly now and under her breath. Her brow, knotted in the manner of the great theorists, as an equation is formulated and then picked apart. It is for her own sake that she stands there and continues to debate with herself, aware that two cups of hot milk have done their work, allowing you to soften into the leather chair and sleep.

I CONTINUE TO LOOK at a partially formed canvas; fragile and imprecise. Just one untruth will ruin it: if I lie to myself, the painting will dissolve. The temptation to destroy clings to my skin, densely packed and impermeable. What painting is, is the temperance and determination to avoid these urges. I am only as strong as my will allows, only measuring my worth in the oil slicks I swim around; the fires I put out.

I sleep in the studio over three nights, as the creature slowly becomes a thing that cannot be left. Its presence in my head has fast-set. The puzzle of its ever-shifting mass governs with an iron rule. A dictatorship of my making; something that both pleasures and sickens. If the creature is to remain with me, standing before my bed as I pitifully attempt sleep, his face behind the mist on my bathroom mirror, my commitment needs to be demonstrated beyond pure thought. It demands a night vigil from my studio chair. With the presence of a desk light, rust eating through its enamel insides, it makes itself known to me. Without the light, he becomes clearer still: your eyes piercing through the black.

The reveal can be archeological in its time frame. I am certain of what I see, but to be sure of what lies beyond, I must wait. Painting requires the hard and physical strength of a master craftsman, coupled with the openness of a diviner. Also, someone who has an understanding of prayer, whether it is reviled or adhered to. I am all of these things before I am myself. It is what the creature demands before he is willing to step completely from the dark.

IN A HOUSE not unlike the one you have run from, they feed you and launder your clothes. You pay your keep by sweeping leaves from the driveway, clearing cobwebs and detritus from the gate. Trading upkeep for upkeep is all that you know. Chuck sleeps for most of the morning – a pill – giving you the run of the house. Only when you see the rows of photographs lining the top of the piano in what he calls the parlor, do you realize how old he is, that he matches your father's age. Fighting in the same wars. What he offers is paternity rather than mere benevolence. It gives you the feeling of safety as you sleep; the tapping of a previously cherished comfort that has been left to run dry for years.

Your breakfast is served by Laurel, who chose to sleep in a guestroom rather than return home. Her familiarity with the kitchen suggests she is more than a passing visitor: cupboards arranged to her liking; food stocked as expected.

– You were expecting servants? So was I. The old man's too mean for that. He'd rather spend his money on a statue with half the plaster cracked off than on a maid's wages. He has me, anyway. I'm the all-in-one. There's a girl who comes three times a week – or would do, if he didn't keep sending her away.

Once it is clear that Chuck is awake, protracted coughing, footsteps above going back and forth over themselves, Laurel disappears to see to the museum.

– His master's voice! Look after yourself.

Her brevity reflects the self-consciousness that a fresh pair of eyes brings, studying their relationship anew; taking stock of the stories she has told: late-night phone calls not being entirely that at all, but tears shed over his bed; shouting dissatisfaction from the bottom of the stairwell. Later you discover that the second guestroom is never used.

Chuck himself is refreshed and energized, forcing your steps a beat faster as you follow him into the cellar. You walk along pathways flanked by banks of sealed crates, pallets double your height that brush the floors above. The greater space is not above the house, you realize, but below it.

Oscar, friendly but unobtrusive, is there to meet you when you reach your destination, along the far reaches of the grounds. As he did when he held open the car door at the steps of the museum last night, he asks after your health, and whether you have everything you need. He stands behind the pair of you patiently as you walk along, well versed in the mechanics of age. Ready to compensate in strength for whatever your bodies lack.

The look that passes between the men suggests that everything has been planned ahead.

– It's where I said it was?

– More or less.

– And you've opened it?

– Taken the sheeting off. The chippings need to be replaced if we have any in the store.

– You can do that afterwards. I'm anxious to show our guest here the beauty we've hoarded.

Before you fell asleep in your unfamiliar bed, you momentarily fooled yourself that you were here for Chuck's hospitality; a reward for being locked in the museum while Laurel went to fetch him. At breakfast you similarly stuck to this delusion: that all you had been looking for was bed and board, and a ride to the train station once an up-to-date timetable could be found. That you had seen all you needed to see in Kentucky. Now, in the cool of the cellar, insulated from damp and wired with rows of spotlights, you feel an anticipatory twist in your guts that makes light work of your previous excuses.

You breathe the same air as in the studio, when we are all at the lumbering turn that leads to finish, fast and shallow. Your palms are wet with the torture of the unknown, weighted with responsibility by a work that has not come from your hand. You feel ready to become my representative in Kentucky, and if need be my defender. You are ready to fight your way out. But what you want most of all is to see it.

The painting is smaller than the others, no more than two feet high and half that in width. It is unframed, though you remember it being held with cream mortise-work – austere Tudor roses in each corner – when you last saw it at a group show of American painters in Washington soon after it was completed. Other than that it is intact.

What strikes you even before you take in how much of your far younger self it depicts – so much so that it feels in many ways closer to youth than manhood – is the vividness of color; a warmer, brighter palate that was long since abandoned, disturbed as I was by criticism which included the words *homespun*, *nostalgic* and *all-American*. So your first glimpse as Oscar pulls it from the box with some care and ceremony reminds you of my weakness, proof that there was a time when the judgment of others could bring me to my knees. To see those colors again is to be reminded of warm blood and impetuousness; a temper that cursed naysayers to high heaven. Under the spotlights, where the unremitting glare heats your face, you relive them again.

You are sitting upright in the studio chair wearing a pair

of denim overalls they gave you for working in the fields. The denim is lightly washed but not worn in any particular place. Its overall hue remains deep, its yellow cinched double stitching luminous against the blue, contrasting with your hair and eyes, both youthful in their luster. Though your face is clean, mud smears your chest and knees, and there is redness to your fingers, indicating foraging of some kind. Your face itself is tilted at an angle so that your gaze does not meet mine. Your hair is smoothed down and parted; that, along with the pose, suggests a conventional vanity portrait or studio photograph, for in spite of your clothes you look at your best: twenty-two and on the cusp of what would follow; as if all that was holding you back from an adulthood of promise was the skein from drying oil paints. Except, in your left hand you hold a furred animal paw of some kind, and your expression is sorrowful. More than that, the act of sitting looks painful, as if every moment in the chair holds an unseen discomfort. Depending on the various ways that a spectator may look here, the fresh face does something to hide it. They can lose themselves in the ruddy cheeks and the wave in your hair parting, and see a celebration of physicality fulfilled; of the primacy of men's toil in the fields. Or they could look harder for the glaze in the eyes and the slight twist to the mouth; the fullness of the lips pulled taut, as something unspoken is swallowed or held back. All that cannot be explained by paint.

– This has been in two sets of hands, this baby. But it's had some bad luck attached, which is why I've never been inclined to show it. I'm not superstitious, per se; more that I wouldn't unknowingly want to hex any folks who happened to see it and feel something for it. There's a responsibility to owning these pieces. You have to decide what is and isn't appropriate. Not in terms of morality, you understand, because I don't judge in that way. But the history of what happens to a painting after it's been sold; that, I pay attention to. One owner killed himself in the same room it was hung in. Another's wife pretended it had been burned rather than lose it in a divorce settlement. I keep it because I love it. Beauty and an awareness of civic duty are not incompatible. What I see before me speaks greatly.

He sees how redness has flooded your face.

– You understand that I can talk about your beauty, son, without it having to mean anything? I'm not one of those types you need to run away from. This is how things are if you're in the game. I appreciate you no differently than I do my cattle that they try to under-price at the county fair. You're both meat. You move with the dollar.

The skin that is visible goes no lower than the base of your neck. The sleeves on the overalls have been rolled up to the elbows, showing the field of hair on your forearms. Everything else about physicality is implied: the fullness in your buttoned chest, the fit of the cloth across your shoulders and thighs. It explains how field work is shaping your body; that this is only one stage of a work in progress. This is what it means to show promise when the end is too distant to be fathomed. It is what this painting is called: *A Promise*.

– You know what this painting is? Un-ob-tain-able. There are museums and dealers all over the country, in Europe and Japan also, who can't get their hands on this and it drives them crazy. Five or six letters come every year. I keep them all. 'We kindly request permission to borrow . . .' 'My client is extremely keen to locate one of the key earlier works by . . .' They scour cellars to look for these babies; read the death notices and news of disasters on the stock exchange. They find what they need, too. Persistence, rugged persistence until it becomes bullying gets these people what they want. I know, because I too can have sly ways. You don't get raised country without learning something. But when they look at their treasure, there's an absence. The piece they really need is missing. Without this painting to explain the others, all that's left to display is greed. Clearly, this isn't the piece that's going to get the paying visitors through the door. It's not the showstopper: the girl with the pert breasts and high derrière at the Moulin Rouge. But to the people who know about these things, it's the clasp that sets the diamond. And the fact that it's not in their club, that they have to travel all the way to a two-horse town in Kentucky to beg for it, kills them. It kills them!

– Something you enjoy, I take it?

– I'm an understanding man. I champion the arts. I champion knowledge. This is what I've given my life to. But, heck, the patronizing tone they stoop to address me in – as if I'm a farmer who just got lucky, who found a stash of paintings in the cow shed that turned out to be good. It takes a lifetime to build a collection. It becomes a message you wish to send. Something bigger than your life. They seem to think that we shuck corn and handle the art in the style of a traveling fair. Canvases smelling of over-boiled hot dogs and burnt cotton candy that sticks in your throat. Lady in the front booth pushing root beer as hard as she's selling tickets.

– That'd be Laurel.

– Well, Laurel's had her fair share of gimmickry, I'll grant you that. Costumes and pageants, and schooling in funny voices to keep the elementary kids hooked. We can't be icy like the Guggenheim or the Tate in London, where you take your chances in those drafty rooms and fend for yourself. We work hard to engage. Laurel busts her balls to get those kids through the door.

Everything you turn against is in those gimmicks. You

would run for miles on seeing merchandising in museum shops; less about those institutions making money from your face, more that there were so many versions of yourself to see. Did each sale diminish something of you, like a photograph taken multiple times, or was it just the sheer scale of them: face after face racked along the wall in the postcard display? Similarly you had a low opinion of the base caricatures that could sometimes be found in the weekend editions.

– If they don't like pictures, they shouldn't make a mockery of them. That's too easy, to make fun of those who choose not to defend themselves; who see nothing to defend. If they can take shots at people just for working hard, then we should be able to do the same.

This was after another incident in the village store, where a sulfurous egg was cracked against the side of my neck. You were facing in another direction and missed it; simply out of your range. Your anger at doing so, failing so publicly, turned you into a defender. You had spent your first few years at the house bathing in its peacefulness, unaware of how what we did affected the environment beyond. Once the rotten egg ran down my back, you were ready to restore the tenets of your Hudson upbringing: fight those who needed to be fought.

– Your Anna's work is validated by museums and collectors, and rightly so. Greatness should be venerated during a person's lifetime. We should appreciate what we have.

– It will change when she dies. They'll forget so much about how those paintings came about. The contributions that were made. It'll boil down to the work that sold for the most money. The Nudes that hang in respectable homes. It's something I need to see for myself before then. Not validation so much, not from those people, at least. I just want to see the paintings and understand whether it was all worthwhile.

– For that we'll need to swap eyes. You're not an outsider, son. You can never know the true value of what you've done.

– I can try.

– Now, indulge me. The rabbit's paw you're holding. That's a novelty of sorts. She steers clear of props usually. It's another reason why this one is such a talisman, because no one can quite understand it.

– A dog's paw. If it was a rabbit, it would be half that size. Maybe even smaller.

Chuck steps closer and then back from the canvas several times, adjusting his gaze. In repose his face loses much of its earlier form and vigor, showing his true age in the slack jaw and lowered eyes. He is conserving the energy to speak again, but it feels as if the room is suddenly awash with tiredness, that little else will come now that he has shared his ideas.

– We had dogs at the farm, but I never had them in the house. Can you believe that? Too much shit on the carpet. I'd have picked up on that if I had been around them more. Spent less time with these crates and my obsession to buy. I know what it is. I don't hide from that word. I've had enough people tell me to my face as well as behind it. 'Chuck, you need to stop spending your money this way and act serious. If you can't find a woman healthy enough to bear your children in this town, go someplace where you will. Bring a family back here. Raise them in your house.' By which they mean, spend the money their way, on whatever nonsense preoccupies them: car ports and motor homes, holidays in Baton Rouge. You put your energies elsewhere after a time. But here, we have a mystery solved. A dog's paw. Why did I never think of that?

Color returns to his face as he talks about painting; always when he talks about painting. Away from it, a hollowness to his features returns. The crates feed his curiosity, restoring his vitality to a level you did not predict. He pats you hard on the back now, laughing; a shake or two of the shoulders as if to wake you up.

– This tickles me. It truly does. To think that those educated folks from the big institutions, with their wire-frame glasses and their fingers up their asses; that the studious buyers for the private collectors more wealthy than I, the ones who would sell their grandmothers still sleeping in their beds if it meant acquiring a rare painting; their clients who would die without seeing absolutely their entire range of acquisitions in full, people for whom the notion of owning could be more important than actually seeing, none of those people picked up that it was a dog's foot. Not one! That every single condescending letter sent to me on the subject mentioned a rabbit's foot. I'll be smiling about this all day. All week! Those bastards. I have the painting and the secret. They'll need to triple their price to get through the door.

He pulls his arm tightly around yours; comrades against the greedy and untrue. You are under no further pressure to speak, both of you studying the painting while reaching for your respective rewards. You understand that he will not ask you more because this is secret enough: a vindication of his beliefs, something that will keep him active for another year. You look at the paw flat in your palm as if an offering: stout and tawny, its fur flecked with black and gold. You think of the afternoon the painting was started, when Vishni shouting in the kitchen pulled me away from the sketch I was working on. You standing over the kitchen table with a dead dog in your arms, hit by a farm cart on the back road.

– I couldn't leave him lying there. I didn't know what to do.

– My God, this animal! This poor animal! My God!

– Sit in the studio. You'll be calmer there. All this shouting isn't a help.

Vishni was angry enough to strike me, both for the insult and because she could read the selfishness of my actions where you could not. All you could see was an animal who would not move. Her cries continued but I turned away once I had spoken because our eyes could not meet. We would be brawling over the table otherwise.

– The heart no longer exists in the people of this world. Oh, this poor animal. Anyone who can leave a dog like this, they have no soul there.

The dog's crown and eyes were wet with blood, caked to his fur like a thick cream shampoo that was yet to be washed away. His coat was matted with it. Overcome with your and Vishni's frenzy, I wondered whether he should be placed in the bath and rinsed under the warm tap; that a spell of water and some vigorous scrubbing would clear the color away. A residual warmth still radiated from the part of his trunk that I could get close to, for you were still clutching him too tightly for either of us to examine him further. The warmth was a trick, as temporal as his last breath. He was clearly dead, and to take him to the bathroom would be to engage in a hopeless ritual that had no place here. You hadn't moved from where you stood by the kitchen table, oblivious to my presence as I tried once more to examine the dog. You kept him tight within your arms as if he were part of you. Vishni rubbed your shoulder gently, as if to make you give way, but you would not yield. Your body seemed to be shutting down in a phantom response, muscles turning rigid as the animal's blood cooled then coagulated. Soon the pair of you would be as stone.

– Come to the studio. Sit in your chair. You don't have to give him to us, but you could sit down, at least. Make him comfortable.

– I'm fine as I am.

But still you followed me to the back of the house.

– He's Edwin's dog. From Ridge Farm.

You are incapable of giving further information, your mouth, the neurons that carry messages to your mouth, closing down in shock. It is days later before we understand how you found him, walking back from the village. Pleased with yourself because there were pats of fresh apple butter on the store counter, and you bought a couple for Vishni, thinking it would surprise and please her. How there was also a packet of cigarettes for me, so that I wouldn't see the butter and complain. You'd started to notice how I could get sometimes when you praised Vishni. How you were full of yourself on account of your foresight. Thinking how much of a man you were for being able to put out fires before they were lit – which was when you saw him, pushed under the hedgerows, two miles from where he should have been on Edwin's farm. Lord knows why he ran so far. Whoever hit him, knowingly or otherwise, settled him in a hurry because his legs were sticking out. It's what you talked of the most. Mottled paws peeping from under the hedge, thinking that it must be a rabbit shot but uncollected. You had no idea what you would find. The way of the farm was still new to you; not yet understanding that attachments

120

for any of the animals, whether working or livestock, were to be avoided unless you wanted poverty or heartache. Your eyes blazed with this ignorance. You did not want to hear about these rules.

– Edwin needs to be called. He'll be wondering.

– Vishni knows how to reach him. Sit down here. Please, sit down.

You looked at me as if I had absorbed nothing. Something new in your face: a harking back to your Hudson upbringing, where those who were misunderstood had to find ways to make themselves heard. We were still at the stage where the difference in our ages was obvious and unwelcome in the attention that it could receive. The disdain from a misunderstood child is no reason to fear, but your bulk continued to loom over me and I was scared of you then. Your look set upon me, intending to wither and decay. The same face would radiate a week later when I made the mistake of bringing a farm puppy to the house, arrogantly assuming that such a simple purchase would heal you. There was much you were capable of until I remembered myself, knowing that nothing would happen while you were still unprepared to put down the dog.

– You'll be no use to Edwin if you don't sit down. Please, John. If you want to go over there.

How wide your eyes were. How quickly your resentment dropped; still so young and so transparent. I could see the blood racing through you.

– We should go to Edwin's?

– Not now. When Vishni's got hold of him. As you say, he might be out with the truck, in which case he won't be home until late.

– Finley's a good, friendly dog. Jumps for apples. Likes his belly tickled. If they knew him, they wouldn't have left him under the bush like that.

– Sit. You'll feel better, I promise you.

Experience is what makes you bow. Sooner or later you have to trust someone who knows a little more. This is how it was, in the beginning at least. Later there is none of that. You will continue to do as you are told, but the simple way that you acquiesce will be lost; in its place comes something firmer and unknown. If there is a moment to pinpoint, it begins with this day when you sit in your chair and I begin to sketch you and the dog while we wait to hear from Vishni. Flint appears and then retreats in your eyes as the animal stiffens; the glossy blood on his coat mattifying as it dries, turning from crimson to rust as the afternoon passes. Your stink is greater than Finley's. Your smells are the alive ones: tears, sweat and piss. Nothing comes from Finley bar metallic blood notes. His body is still doing its work before it can settle into rot.

We stay there until dark. You sit. I draw. This is all we know. The dog dissolving into your arms the harder you hold him. He tucks and folds, his body turning in on itself, as if to tidy himself away is the last thing he can do; a gesture to make your experience easier to bear. Showing a selfless-ness that I am unable to show, because I am too concerned with finishing what I need to before the light fades.

I SLEEP MORE; some of this involuntarily. Vishni feeding me things to ensure that I have the energy to work. We no longer sit and talk outside. Days when the only times I see Ben are inside the studio. The understanding that your body is being depleted; that you are a hostage to what will and won't function is a specter impossible to shake. I have trained to find it in Vishni before I see it in myself. The effort it takes her to complete the stairs; the trips to the village becoming less frequent, even if a taxi is offered to take her; that her sketching has dwindled to nothing. If I look closely I can see that the house is not as clean as it was; sunlight at different times of day showing a patina of dust across furniture and atop frames. A footprint at the bottom of the refrigerator where someone has kicked the door closed; flowers drying in their vases, while the water that holds them grows milky. Every difficulty is understood. Ben has been seen with a mop and bucket, helping Vishni, each of them tackling opposite ends of the room, racing to see who will meet the other first. In the country, our ways of making fun are different. Ben rolls with what he finds here: chores, play, sit for the painting. We are all in bed by eight thirty; dead to the world by nine.

I worry that I have neglected Vishni; aware of the heaviness in her movements since you left, but helpless to offer anything practical, clumsy in my gestures to make her laugh.

How to lighten the mood, when everything that illuminates is extinguished? Ben has been a temporary and welcome salve, but he too has retreated into himself, absorbed into the mechanics of finishing the painting. A feeling of brood-iness has infused. They are joined together by this. They whisper softly to each other in the kitchen; snatched moments when it is presumed that I am out of earshot. They make plans, both new to this; having to prepare for events; taking care of something that had long been assumed would be handled by you. This doesn't excuse their amateur-ishness, that they are unable to be truly quiet; how certain phrases – *She mustn't know; They're examining everything, every deed, every file* – are expelled from their mouths and trapped in bubbles that mingle with the paint fumes. Words captured but rising out of reach. If there were more energy filling each cell, I would tear those bubbles apart. I would scrub the floors and dust cobwebs from every cornice until they caught in my hair and throat. I would hoard all papers out of their reach, burning those that needed to be burned. I would strike those who disrespected or tried to mother me, remembering what I'd been taught as a young woman on the streets of Jersey Heights: you cannot defend yourself if you never look up.

But what energy I have must go on the painting. This is not the time to divide what reserves I have. In stronger periods, work would always come before the practical and considered: paint before birthdays, funerals, bills.

– You choose not to celebrate.

An observation from Vishni, the week before a nearly forgotten birthday had occurred.

– You don't know how. It makes you uncomfortable.

Similarly, you could cut me cold.

– You hide behind your paintings. They get you out of things you don't want to do. One of the farmers on the other side of the river missed the birth and death of both his children because the cows needed to be milked, when no milk meant no money. You're no different.

Painting is an ongoing act of revelation. There is nothing that I hide behind. If I excuse myself from anything it is only because I know that, if I am taken away from the work, then nothing but that fills my head. I am struck dumb; obtuse by most standards. In the midst of parties it is silence that I most crave. Daylight, silence, the discomfort of my room where the chair has gone years waiting to be reupholstered; the oil burner only giving out half the heat it should do. (To feel truly warm you must step inside the kitchen where the heat from the stove thaws stiff joints and colors pallid lips.) This is what I return to, what is dreamt of and fought over. Arguments about the hours spent in this room taking more time than those requiring that I defend my work. Stating your beliefs to an invisible mass is no act of bravery in this context. Writing a letter to the *New York Times* to defend Vishni's picture from hundreds of complaints after its publication took no longer than half an hour. I stated facts. I was firm in my emphasis on the importance of portraiture; that it should be truthful; that the beauty the complainants wished for should be sought elsewhere. No hand-wringing was involved. No blood on the page.

But a late afternoon one summer, when the light was still strong and bold, when it praised everything it touched, promising growth for all that could be grown, and making true its intent that all that was wounded could be healed. When you stood outside the window and asked me to hike upstream, a rucksack packed with food as a surprise, your trunk pulsing from excitement with the pre-intentioned energy of the young. How long you had studied my routine, planning on the right time to do this, not understanding that to reveal cannot be measured on the factory clock; that

125

what must be wrestled with cannot be left to the next day. You didn't understand when I shouted at you, sending you away to hike with Vishni, when I could have easily set down my things and changed into my walking shoes. On a beach in Provincetown, you tried to get me to dance by the fire of wood and shingle, only to be pushed away, because something in the movement of fireflies was greater. You were filled with the same impulsiveness then; the desire to pull me out of myself. It was a simplicity I should have allowed.

Battling with this painting is how I atone. Sitting in the near dark as Vishni and Ben brew tea and have their conversations is what is expected of me. Something must be produced to account for my behavior; something to be shared inevitably comes from a selfish hand.

– I'm thinking we should take her to New York before she gets too frail. There'll be some colors she's after. Maybe something in the permanent collection at MoMA or the Guggenheim will call her, if we jog her memory of what is there. She needs to see St John and it will be easier if we pass by his office.

– He's never been here. There's never been a reason for him to be here.

– That's why I haven't invited him down. If we're just passing by his office en route to somewhere, it'll seem like a chance thing.

– She doesn't believe in chance. Only in what's planned. She'll hear it in our voices. See the nervousness in our hands.

– Possibly. But the city will have much to distract her. The noise and the paintings. A few places to have good food.

– We're speaking of a child. This is how you treat a child who cannot be controlled.

– There is only pragmatism in what we're doing. There's business she needs to address in New York. This is the easiest way to get her there.

Everything spoken in the house comes to me; porous wood and stone; threadbare curtains through which words can escape. Fury, worry, mockery reach this room. All the emotions that cannot be shown.

The last time Vishni was in the city was when you took her five years ago, as the last series of paintings were close to completion. I was harder on you than I had been previously; frustrated with the pace of the work, ready to strike out at any perceived signs of complacency. Eighteen months of strictness and rages wearing down to a single fiber the loyalty that bound us together.

– You've put both of us through the wringer. Rolled us out until we're as flat and faded as carbon copies.

There was scarcely any life between you; eyes that struggled to stay open, muscles fighting the urge to slacken into repose, their memory forcing stringency to your posture when it was clear you were ready to buckle. Twenty minutes of rest, sometimes an hour, was nothing; the torture was returning to the pose, before the creation of another, and another.

– You've said this is the end for now – let it be so. Now it's our turn to do as we please, find some pursuits that will plump us out, shake off what has crushed us.

Two weeks. I wouldn't give a day longer, too anxious to allow you to be absent when the final touches to the paintings needed to be made; those last flashes of clarity that only come from a period away from the work. Enlightenment generated from the guilt I feel when I am not using my hands.

You camped in the Catskills and hiked for several days. Living like boy scouts on cans of franks and chili beans. You chased raccoons away from the campsite, snarky animals whose irritability was as great as their hunger, and swam among the silver-threaded fish that populate the lake at the bottom of the mountains. Each day you hiked fifteen or twenty miles further east toward the road that would eventually lead to New York. You were never happier than on one of these trips. The freedom you felt simply from being away from the house and having mountain dust in your shoes.

Vishni knows this. She's always known this. She agrees to travel with you because she understands the darkness of my mood when I am still so encased by paint; that for me to be in an environment where you have mastery is difficult to take. How it makes me wonder where my own mastery lies, and its value. Whether I have accurately captured all the expressions you show outside the studio; the pleasure that's radiated when a school of silver fish swims between your legs, the satisfaction that fills you when you reach the top of the mountain. The shock on Vishni's face as the wind rattles past her as you stand on the cliff ledge; the way it pushes against the loose skin on her face. This, the element you both hold in reserve, is what ensures canvas after canvas. Reactions that come from nowhere, needing to be painted; an expression in the eyes and lips hinting at a pain I hadn't foreseen.

I am kept company. The house echoes with your failings. The threats I make when you're unable to sit still. Shards of glass from an upturned beaker, after you were roused from a sleep you did not wish to leave, remain scattered around the sink. I stopped Vishni clearing it – or you, late in your repentance – because the reminder is a sound one: of the paintings I cannot get right. I spend five days drawing the glass before I leave for New York; crumbs atop newspaper; shards that glitter beyond the muck caked across the sink mouth. I am drawing your hand: what it is capable of. Even when you're not here, what you contribute dominates my mindset; maybe more so, because without distractions all I have are habits to fall back on. An old dog that cannot learn anything new.

Riding the night train; deserted carriages whose smell speaks of the day's passengers. I think of the darkness of the boxcar that first brought you here: the occupants crammed within it; the rankness that pounded your nose and mouth. Hands that roamed over your body while you slept. Searching for money, liquor and other things. Twenty years old. Looking younger. Were you afraid of what you found there? Was there hope among those riding into the country, or only expectation of the same? A sickening sensation that grew familiar: cars close to knocking into one another as a train in the opposite direction ran by; deafened by the sudden multiplication of steel on steel; the thunder of wheels pushing forward; how the air in the narrow space between the two trains seemed to have been sucked out. You saw the faces of those in other boxcars, those men fleeing the unyielding farmlands for a life in the city, which they were told would promise more. Did they have the same determination as the folk who shouldered you, or the same dread?

Buffeted by the smoothness of an electric line, and the studious attention of the purser, I am cosseted in comfort and warmth. No night terrors to keep me from sleep, as you may have had; accustomed to the emptiness of my surroundings, and the dark. Yet on seeing my reflection in the glass I understand that I am not quite immune: a ghost floating in the split navy of the countryside speeding past.

Walking through the city; ten blocks to awaken my senses. Feeling the comfort of the dark. Always the darkness I prefer here. Most shops closed. Diner signs flashing across the street; their beacon clear. Lighthouses in an urban jungle. The sound of my tread as I walk across littered streets. Heels catching on newspaper. Needles on the stairwell as I leave the station. The insulation of a cab ride would feel pacifying when I do not wish it to be so. Something of the native in my steps, as if I was born with the pull of the Hudson rushing through my ears. Channeling the shift in your posture that happens when you return here, but not realizing this until later: the stiffening of your back and jutting of your chin; how your eyes appear sharper, ready to react.

No suitcase to speak of, yet still breathless after two blocks. The luggage that is being sent on ahead, with the cab I chose not to ride in, may as well be carried on my back I am bent so; my head has dropped to my chest for how hard I am made to push for breath. There have been flashes before: running through the meadow to find my errant sitter before the sun disappears; a light-headedness that outstayed its welcome on descending a ladder while fixing a canvas. This, however, is the first time the force of my lungs seems beyond the realm of my control. I have no power over its efficacy; must simply stand and wait for the tightness to pass; to be patient and not fight myself; to override panic and fool myself that I will be somehow rewarded if I can accept these shallow breaths as a trail to more substantive function. Shallow will lead to deep. Warmth shall radiate through my chest if I stay calm and allow it.

What comes to me is an exchange between you and Vishni before the paintings were finished, an exchange that I blocked out. Words that can disappear all too easily if I pull harder on the charcoal that glides across the page, or turn the faucet open a fraction more. Except my ears never close completely. The desire for knowledge is too great, both inside the house and out. In these years, curiosity can be the strongest rope you have in keeping you alive.

– She gets tired, in case you didn't notice. Needed help to lift the canvas the other day. That's never happened before.

– She was being difficult because she couldn't get her own way. Playing with us because I spent an hour shucking corn when I was meant to be here.

131

– It seems more than that. The rest she's talking about is as much for her as it is for us. She wants to hibernate.

This is the moment I can pinpoint, when I realize that my body has changed.

You are having a drink at the hotel bar as I arrive. Still framed by your country trek, your face is sunburnt and hair wiry from bathing in the river, but there is no trace on Vishni, as if the physicality of the week has been an act of the imagination. Her skin remains pale, hair swept back into a bun as if it had never been uncoiled the entire trip. My impulse is to shed my coat and join you; that if I pull up a chair I can talk, and have my blood-ways washed through with alcohol, I can make good a body that has let me down. Resetting the system without having to make a declaration or medical visit of any kind.

I have never been so interested to hear about camping. To hear about things that have nothing to do with the room I trap you in. But instead comfort comes here, as I stand in the lobby and watch you. Easier to watch; waiting for my chest to settle and the redness to leave my face. Never realizing that I would fear the things that used to make us strong.

FLUID, ALL THAT FLOWS between us. How we share the same surname and allow people to assume. How we share the same hotel room and allow people to assume. We believe it ourselves sometimes. Country marriage: no paperwork; only the evidence of your eyes. Matching rings, bought on a trip to California. This closeness that cannot be challenged.

Our marks are interchangeable; flitting back and forth like moths across the cracked night-light. You are more likely to rinse your cup after you have used it, but we both leave it in the same place, on the left side of the table rather than on the drainer. We are both guilty of taking food in the night, usually that which Vishni has determined be eaten the next day; hefty, imprecise shapes cut from pies; legs torn from a chicken carcass.

– You're animals. I should leave you to eat from cans and pull vegetables from the mud and horseshit.

In the same way, your hand has crossed each painting, as if it is my body depicted on the canvas. These brushstrokes are shaped by your will, especially those days when I feel that I have directed nothing; that I am merely a cipher for your control. My hand moves repetitively, as paint is layered thickly to hide your secrets; tears streaming from the stench of turps, unable to breathe or think. It is only as I clean up afterwards that I see the way you look at me and realize my mistake. For you it is the other way around. You understand that your position is to sit and surrender everything. The guilt is in my mind.

How often does our perception shift? On which days does who blame whom? For this reason I no longer recognize paintings in chronological terms. All I see is mood and balance: which of us held the greater power over that particular painting; who was victorious.

You were restless in Santa Ana, wanting to move with the winds. The day indulging our hosts at the museum was a torture for you, still learning to understand that the paintings followed us everywhere, and how to lodge them in the back of your mind. Once our obligations were over, before the warmth of their parting handshakes was yet to leave us, you pulled me by the elbow and ran.

You drove us into the desert to escape the town. You had latent energy to expend from holding your tongue, so you filled the car with talk as we sped across asphalt into shimmer and rust.

– They were in a spin about those casts, weren't they? You'd think they'd never seen metal rings before. One of them actually squeaked when you praised them, did you hear? Like an excited little mouse waiting for his Art to arrive. Then they were all at it, because each had to demonstrate their enthusiasm in some way. An orchestra of mice. Rushing about your casts as if they were cheese.

Even with the roar of *eee eee eee* pounding your ears, a cacophony of rampaging mice, you still allow yourself room to think; somewhere to sit and block the smallness of it all, and smile graciously when eyes stray back to you.

Relaxed as you were, your shoulders fell softly as you held the steering wheel, creating a line I often found hard to achieve in the studio. The desire to stop in the dust, for you to hold that pose was overwhelming. I thought of grabbing the steering wheel or pulling the keys from the ignition. It was perfection that could only be briefly held. Nor could I draw your attention to it, how perfect you were, for the afternoon was yours. I had no right to ask anything.

– I sat thinking about the sun rising this morning; how I saw it cross the arc of the hotel garden before settling across the town's skyline. I misjudged how long it would take. At home, dawn is a flash, as fast as a blind being pulled up. Shop's open; time for work. Here it seemed to take for ever. Everything in the garden revealed so slowly, like a mystery unraveling, until finally both it and Santa Ana became clear. Now there's no difference to how the sun draws back and illuminates us. Any fool can tell you that, the inevitability of the sun falling and rising again. But this morning, I felt so insignificant in its scale. A snail tracing a path across the damp paving; me standing in my underwear on the hotel balcony. No difference. These are not great discoveries, but this was how I felt, and no matter how small that was, it was still something greater than when I stood in front of those metal rings. It was clearly the artist's idea of a joke, yet they accepted it as something real. They hide from life, these museum people. Something has happened to each of them to have built a barrier where they can redefine the world. They are good people, some of them, but two days in their company is enough. A vacation from our life.

There is no getting away from what a desert town is: poorly lit, over-hospitable, melancholy. You checked us into the highway motel, threadbare but clean, with color TV and a kidney-shaped swimming pool out back, clouded emerald with chlorine. The chemicals in the water were stronger than exhaust fumes from the highway, its scent coated the back of our throats and settled into the lower pockets of our lungs. We could taste the swimming pool for weeks afterwards.

You took my hand and walked up Main Street – the day was defined by your hand pulling mine – confident of your navigation, following a self-devised trail that led past a stream of clapboard stores that needed our window study: the general store, a bookstore and a jeweler's. Your eyes set off sparks in a way that made me want to stop you in your tracks again. Even a photograph could not have done justice to the smile across your face; how you glowed, so sure of yourself.

While ham and eggs were frying in the diner, you disappeared, claiming to have dropped your silver comb in the store. Your movement was sudden and definite as you stood to check your pockets, interrupting the waitress attempting to sell slices of a muddy pumpkin pie that sat on the counter. The food arrived, cooled, and then congealed. You were retracing your steps, going back further than the store, taking in the gas station, the church; the meandering dust trail that lay between them and the motel. Coffee became my meal, and when I was too hungry to wait, a fresh plate of food. The waitress was nonplussed. This wasn't the first husband she'd seen who ran out on his wife. Whether eaten or not eaten, every scrap she wrote on her order pad was billable.

I was eating when you returned; the ceremony of waiting had long since passed. We share these peasant tendencies, for when I'm hungry, I eat. Complex needs best solved by simplicity: bread, for hunger; paint, for everything else. This is what makes sense; the route I've always taken. People can never lose themselves this way. Running on the same logic, you took your opposite seat in the booth, a bread roll in your hand and a small square box on the table: two problems solved.

– You're not the only one who was thinking about rings today.

– What's this?

– John Brown. Anna Brown. We just put them on before we leave. Easiest thing.

– You want to stop their questions.

– How they look at you, in the museum and elsewhere. They should be looking at the paintings. Nothing else.

Bravery masked your fear; the tools of your tender age. You sat solidly, but your eyes darted with nerves, a fine trail of sweat framing your cheeks and hairline. I was old enough to warn you away, push you toward something better, for a tie, even an imaginary one, would take hold and tighten, choke; once the ring had been taken for granted by those on the outside, we would still be bound. If I held your gaze for longer I might have discerned that this was precisely what you wanted; for me to put a stop to your impulsiveness, dismissing it as the indulgences of a child. But your body was not that of a child, nor the determination that had settled upon your face. These were your rules to lay down. Everything was decided.

The chink of metal touching metal as your hand covered mine across the diner counter. How that made me feel. The way I bit my lip to stifle any sound. In turn we nodded at the other before settling back to our cold eggs and dinner rolls; something of a Pioneer or Quaker arrangement, where tacit agreement – trust – were the only things needed in the absence of God. Your way of celebrating: chatting with the waitress and asking her to turn up the radio. Benny Goodman followed by Kay Starr. You patted your fingertips against my knee, happily in time, knowing that I could not be pulled onto the floor. The tapping of palms and fingers, mine slowly following yours, was a wedding dance of sorts; harmony through music; still tender as if recovering from an electric shock, but a degree of light-headedness and abandon. The waitress brought out a slice of pie with a candle slipping to an angle in its center.

– Explains why you were looking so sad, earlier. I get like that myself on my birthday. No one to share it with, unless those useless children of mine remember that they have a mama.

We did not feed each other, but the pie was shared: dry at the top and damp at the bottom; an imperfect cake to mark our imperfect wedding. The rings, the dance, the cake: from these barren elements our marriage was created. We ate for real this time, hungry, muddled, pleased with ourselves. Later, back at the motel, further allowances were made. You carried me over the threshold; a country boy, bringing all his traditions to an alien environment. Motel thresholds and gas station flowers. A sense of leadership as the celebrations continued into the night; the husband owning his wife; possession that could not be replicated elsewhere. Muddled from drink and the rush of the day, both thinking of the alternative life: homesteader and bride performing the duties required of them while their wedding party heckled from downstairs. To grow crops and to breed, becoming strong members of their community as their parents had before them. Stifled by duty and a sense of propriety. An assured voice that could never be as strong as the husband's. Lessons drummed into me at the kitchen table as a child. What I had walked away from, for one night I entertained: a dangerous combination of happiness and curiosity, all because you had bought the rings.

You're aware that the animals are being mistreated, but are able to do little from your bed. Nothing you can see, but recognizable sounds; agitation and distress. The kindness they have shown after you collapsed at the truck-stop café, offering their home because the bus driver refused to take you (that it was the responsibility of this couple or the police, because the woman who ran the café refused to wait for you to come round); how attentive they are in their ministrations, how quietly they move around you, the softness of their voices, depletes the energy and care that should be given to the cows in the shed. It is less the animals' vocal protest, more their relentless movement that disturbs your fitful sleep; hooves stamping in the barn, a collective strength that pushes against the walls of the flimsy wooden house in waves; the stench of piss that travels with them.

– Are they happy out there?

– Happy enough. Ignore their hooligan tendencies and rest. We'll see to them shortly.

Whether they are eventually seen to, you are unaware; their lowing sharp and relentless; their feet unable to rest. Surely it should be the other way around – you in your delirium, while they swish their tails in contentment, settled back into their cycle of feed and milking; that even if they are simply cared for rather than loved, there is the certainty of routine that quiets their noise. Instead, you lie in a cot

139

across from the kitchen fire, tender but lucid, while the sway of their bulk in that limited space increases in force.

Your hosts are Haley and Peg, middle-aged and childless; their bodies twisted out of form by the rigors of intensive farming. Symptoms you recognize from closer to home: the overdeveloped shoulders and neck, morphed from years of leading cattle; hands browned and calloused from twice-daily milking; deafness, medical and otherwise. Two decades younger but somehow looking closer to you in age. Their farm sits on Idaho prairie, an undeveloped patch flanked by commercial potato-growers. Your eyes were unable to settle on the landscape as the bus rode through the night; azure and shadow being all that reflected through the glass. Your thoughts were only of Washington and what you would find there: a painting of interest in the Dutch Embassy. One that you don't remember seeing finished, or that your memory blurs with another painting; one sitting shifting into the next. There was a series with fish ten years ago: you with a string of catch pulled from the water that same day; diamond-shaped river trout from whose silver-coal skin light poured as if from a scatter-gun; your hands tight at each end of the line as if they had that same value, precious as jewels. Another: asleep, with a fly poking from your closed fist; part talisman, part comfort blanket. And the last: arriving home at sunrise after Edwin's boy, Wendell, lost his footing in the undercurrent and drowned; showing how, in the space of moments, ten minutes of frantic rescue, and another ten on the bankside, pumping a heart that refused to yield, how a body can be drained of hope.

You are uncertain which painting the Embassy owns; whether its purchase was motivated by an underlying fixation with life or death. Whichever the case, there remains an element from that time which draws you there; paintings that record how you were not yet jaded by your vocation here

– that even after the death of the boy, whether standing on crumbling soil or the damp studio floor, life was everything you wanted it to be. So you must locate the painting in your mind, somewhere between what is real and imagined, as you lie at Haley and Peg's. The chances of you reaching Washington are remote. Energy reserves can be replenished; sleep, whatever comes, can do its job to nurse and erase. The problem lies in your frame and what it can take. Twenty hours on a threadbare bus is more than you can withstand; for although your eyes feed on every inch of the country passed, your body absorbs every inconsistency on the road; each pothole and crack in the asphalt. An airport is to be found three hours away, but this brings more officialdom than you have the patience for. Discomfort will be felt however you journey, it is down to you to equate this with your need to find what needs to be seen; to keep warm and drink plenty of fluids, to remember to eat, and find some way – any – to sleep.

– Boy's Own Adventure, with a Boy's Own mind.

Peg, in summary to Haley, when they assumed he'd fallen to shut-eye.

– Traveling alone with barely a thing on him. I thought they were raised with more sense in the East.

– He can conduct hisself any way he likes, woman. A coat and some good shoes are all you need to get by. He's proof. Men reached the far ends of the country with much less.

– Younger men.

– Not always. When a man has nothing, or needs to provide, he will search and find.

– He doesn't need to provide. He has a credit card. Could stay anyplace.

The card is put under some scrutiny, familiar in these parts, but mostly unwanted. In the mind of Haley and Peg, its owners are primarily showmen and crooks, although not entirely different in disposition to farm people, who can be

141

ugly as the nature they are enslaved to and take care of. The card makes them mistrustful, paying more attention to how much food is eaten and how far you stray into the rest of the house. The bag with the remainder of the money not left for Chuck is sitting in the trunk of the Greyhound Bus that left you behind. The camera is gone too; the thing that hurts the most. This would have been explained to Haley and Peg if they had asked. Instead they took you on sight: a man who traveled without excess weight; his past jettisoned at an earlier destination, along with his luggage.

– Is there a place you be looking to stay? The town has a motel. It isn't nothing special, but they have color TV and pool in the downstairs bar.

– Close to the amenities. Grocery, drugstore, doctor.

– Or the train station, if you have somewhere urgent to be.

A call is made to St John from the post office – credit cards are not the only credentials they disapprove of. Arrangements, your care, is taken from their hands, immediately lightening the mood in the house; misgiving returning to generosity. It has been several days of indecision and worry for your hosts; careful to nourish you, but arguing among themselves who was best qualified to oversee the more intimate ablutions.

– St John asked Peg if you were any weaker.

– He ain't looking like Hercules, but he's better, I told him. The soup's bringing back some color to his cheeks. The apple pie's giving him energy. If he wants to help us milking cows, he'd be in a position to by the weekend.

– The heifers are old now and we can't afford no bulls. We'll milk 'em until they're gone and that's it.

But there is no evidence of the cows being milked; their moans growing blunter and more distant as you slowly begin to block out their sound. Haley and Peg remain close,

142

seldom leaving the house, making you wonder whether it is still the means of your arrival that concerns them, or that you are sicker than you realize. Your care is administered like parents to an infant: round the clock, with the same tone used on calves rejected by their mother. No child had been born in this house. Yours is the first helplessness to emanate from the brittle wooden cot; the human kind; cries that do not come from a bovine mouth. They grow attached and will find it a wrench when you leave.

It is wrong to say that the cows called you, more that you were a frustrated patient who needed to escape confinement. The urge to use your hands, to solve something that could so easily be solved, was too great for you to remain prostrate in a cot built for a child who never arrived. Good intentions thwarted were as much a part of the farm's make-up as the beetle-infested wood and the stench. Unspoken disappointment was the history of this place, from the cartoon-inscribed glassware on the top shelf of the dresser to the furrows that so deeply lined their faces. You felt your body being nourished by the soup as much as by their sadness; how similar furrows would mark your own brow the longer you stayed an invalid. Your footsteps away from the fire were weak ones, tentative, not only from a lack of strength, an inability to move across the kitchen floor with any command (each shuffle and tread informed by a sensation of vertigo), but of being unaware how soon your hosts would return from town. This exercise could not be accomplished under their guidance; its basic nature demands secrecy. At the door you feel the solidity of your legs, a mastery of the sea. The fear of gravity's inevitability – that sooner or later you will lose your footing and fall to the ground – leaves you once you step outside; your senses flooded with too much else: flat, even sunlight; cold air; the dampness of the meadow and the intensely sweet bovine smell coming from the shed.

Something in the heat and filth intoxicates; elements that make your pulse quicken on any farm: surrounded by life, which must be grown, exploited, harvested. Your eyes in the studio, when there is electricity between us, is similar; understanding when your every heartbeat is recorded by my hand. You are weak, and know that, but still you push hard against the barn door; urgency in your movements; greedy to see. Both the animals and yourself take a few moments to adapt to the changing light, theirs to the brightness, yours to the dust and gloom. There are eight of them, all heifers, several seasons past calving. On a city farm they would have more value as meat; sparing three years of milking by driving them to the abattoir on a late autumn morning, and then their carcasses to the butcher. Beef joints for Christmas and Thanksgiving; steaks to see in the New Year. The milk and butter that passes through Haley and Peg's hand is hardly as lucrative. They can churn butter long after the meat has been cooked and eaten, but the logic escapes you, unless they are kept out of sentiment: cattle as much their companions as their livelihood. Other farms would carry argument: younger men, nourished by the same agricultural disappointments as his hosts, but still with fire and fight; wives who toil just as hard as their husbands in fields and milking sheds; an army of skinny children growing around them and learning to do the same. But romance has no place in the countryside of your experience, only an interest in what is right. Pleasure comes from the small rewards gleaned from a job done well: cream in your coffee skimmed off the top of the milk pail; a glut of squash from a weekend harvest; washing your face in the creek before you return to the house. You must work now for your reward, albeit the face of St John and his driver through the darkened glass of the town car as they arrive to take you away.

The shuffling increases once the door is opened; your presence disturbing them more than the light. You feel as if you are inside a wave, pushing yourself upward to find the rip curl, as you walk the gangway that flanks two rows of stalls. I've told you more than once that you are free to leave at any time. If you can be happier elsewhere, find another occupation to fill your heart and mind, then that is where you should be. (Using less thoughtful words than I am here. Calling you lazy, non-committed, stupid, sub-normal; whatever was needed at the time to bring back your fire.) Sitting is neither comfortable nor welcome, but you should still feel the need to do it. The compulsion should be as strong as my will to paint; at times, stronger. You should want to let me speak what you are unable to say. Mostly it has been this way. You are a man of sound mind. You would not stand on the studio floor if you felt it was not worthwhile. What you have long posed for is what you have now become: a man who knows himself and his place in the world. How you have been hewn from the studio chair and from the fields; what you have learned, and what you carry. But you see none of those things as you crouch in the cow shit and start milking, guided by instinct and the memory of your hands; the repeated pattern that thumb and forefinger must follow; the weight applied from the fleshy pad of your palm. You lose yourself to ritual and labor; thoughts of your father unloading sacks of grain at the docks; of late summers shucking corn and cutting cucumbers from tangled vines. The satisfaction of physical work producing something that can be seen. Tangible results from using your hands: a pallet cleared; a cart piled high with trays of apples. This is how they find you, Haley, Peg and St John: ankle-deep in shit with two full pails by your side, refusing to leave until the last cow has been attended to and the final churn filled.

SOMETHING WENT WRONG. I saw it in your eyes. You have lost your borrowed tackle, or let the fish swim away. Edwin was drunker than usual, making the afternoon an unpleasant one. Possibly you took against each other and fought in front of the boy. The limited nature of my thinking only allows these possibilities. The news when you are able to tell it shocks me in two ways: how light-headed I suddenly feel by listening to you and finding the words through the crack in your voice. That a mischievous boy, too scared to set foot inside the house, will never again stand shyly on the porch with his father. Secondly, the realization that everything I know is meaningless in the shadow of the death of a child. The words I speak are trivial to your ears. I cannot hold you the way you wish to be held, with the fierceness of a mother's protective love. It's a failing I have.

 – His pallor when we pulled him out. I knew he was gone just from that. All the color drained from him. Transparent. As if he belonged in the river rather than on land.

 – You need to keep this blanket around you; otherwise you'll make yourself sick.

 – You have to feel something to be sick. I can't feel anything.

 – That's shock. Your body's protecting itself.

– The worst has already happened. It can't protect me from that. What I've had to do.

– I know.

– The sounds Edwin was making as I pumped Wendell's chest. When I knew we'd tried for long enough. Punishing his body unnecessarily when it had already been punished enough.

– You did everything you could.

– Having to drag a father away from his boy. Hostility in his eyes. Pure animal instinct. Determined not to leave him. To protect his son, even though there was no life left within him.

I have nothing to offer, bar the shelter of the couch and the bottle of rye on the window shelf. He is not ready for either, but still too shattered to be herded upstairs. His posture is one of a broken man, uncertain what use he can fulfill after failing what was asked of him. *Save my boy. Bring him round.*

– CONCENTRATE, BEN. I can see that you're losing focus.

– I am focusing, just not on what you want. If I daydream, I forget that my leg has fallen asleep and the spasm running up the side of my neck.

– Unless it's agony, you'll have to stay like that a while longer. I'm not ready for a break yet.

– You never are. Every ten minutes you give me is hard won. During your break you barely sit. Too busy thinking about what comes next. It's endless.

– I'm not sure whether that's praise or criticism. This is what painting is. Or how I work, at least. You know all this.

– This is the complaining part of the program. I'm worn out. I've been thinking about matchsticks all morning; how, if I were to build this house from matchsticks, inside and out, furniture and all, it would still be completed before your painting.

– You've sat for paintings before. You understand that it can be frustrating.

– Sitting would be easy. It's lying on the floor that's hard.

– Ha!

– I posed for you in the early days, before you became a master. This is what I'm realizing. What you ask for. What you expect. There's less precision in other paintings I've sat for. Disciplined, but not with the same rigor.

148

– And how does that make you feel?

– Like being at the bottom of a mine, with the lift being pulled up inch by inch.

– You think that's never happened to John? To Vishni?

– I'm not describing a particularly exclusive feeling. It's frustration that's at the heart of it. And solidarity with those two. Feeling like I've joined the club. I once asked John what he thought about when he was sitting here. 'Everything and nothing,' he said. 'My whole life passes before me when I stand in front of her. Yet at the same time, I'm blank. A space for her to fill.'

– He brings what he brings. Same as you. The rest comes from my hand and eye. What the light gives.

– There's a prison warden hiding inside you, isn't there? Fiddling with those paint tubes rather than jangling keys.

– An open prison. Turn the latch. Walk down the path and push the gate.

– The meadow is their boundary. No one shall pass.

– Not so medieval.

– Well, the house isn't overrun with visitors. Not like it used to be. You have a capsule here where everyone knows their place; how to pull their weight; how the hardest work will be rewarded. You're the captain of a submarine that spends nine months at the bottom of the sea, putting out fires in the belly of your vessel. You curtail willfulness as well as draw it.

– You're testing out your theories on me. Making your mind up how you'll talk about it afterwards.

– Am I getting close?

– Those nights we used to play poker up in Provincetown. Does my face look any different to how it did at your card table?

– I'm sticking to the submarine idea. Something tells me it's a winner.

– They'll want words to go with the pictures, the newspapers.

– In their eyes, paintings cannot be printed with explanation.

– Demystification.

– One and the same. They'll want to know why their readers should look at so many paintings of John and Vishni.

– And why it ends with you.

– That too. First and last.

– There are things we should discuss. Those not possible to sign in New York.

– It doesn't have to be today. If at all.

– Invisible documents. Understandings.

– This you don't have to say. Something you spell out to strangers.

– Like I said. Understandings. That you will speak for me afterwards. Explain but not demystify. Vishni will find her own way to document things. It will come through in her painting. The commentary, all that they demand, will have to come from you.

– And John?

– We don't know where John will be. Wherever he goes, he'll need your explanation too.

– I know.

– The photographs, letters. Use whatever you need. Something similar has been put in writing, but I can't word a document the way I can arrange a contract with you when we're both sitting in the same room.

– I'm lying, not sitting.

– Attention to detail. It's why you're right for the job. Why you're here.

THEY THINK THAT they're the first to get angry; to belittle the process by making faces, or defiantly moving out of position; breaking the furniture that sits within frame when the strength of my reaction is not the one they desire. They believe their sudden exit from the studio will destroy months of work; that my motivation, too, will be decimated by their loss; that I am hostage to their will and tantrums. How I must feed the animal and placate the delusions they hold: their importance within Art; that it is their face which is seen, not my hand; the hand becoming irrelevant in the gallery or auction room. How the face will always take precedence.

Ben's distaste is nothing I haven't seen from you or Vishni. His lapse of manners appearing once frustration takes hold; goodwill evaporating in the heat of the oil fire; the purity of his intentions strangled by the smell of turps that floats heavily in the room, thick like rope. You once carried a ewe into the studio, refusing to take her away; the challenge being that if I was so set on painting life, I should be working with a creature that would not stay still; how I must be afraid of life if I was unable to accurately capture an animal that was bigger than the painting. You were still angry about the dog. This was one of the revenges you waged. There was no gentleness as you pulled her across the studio and dropped her into the chair, not until you registered her

151

distress; understood that nothing was being achieved. You learned that I could not be punished that way; to wound could only come from the pose, that ability to stay perfectly in position while giving nothing of yourself. Relishing the effort it would take on my part to draw you out.

Vishni has tested me in other ways, changing parts of her appearance mid-painting; a forehead suddenly muddy with henna; eyebrows threaded to a series of dashes; her pubis shaved between an evening sitting and one that followed the next morning. Her displeasure at these times no longer remained internalized, choosing instead to physically mark her powerlessness, forcing me to decide whether to include her message in the work, knowing that I could only comply; how it was my duty to record. Twice I have changed the direction of a painting because of her actions; caught in the tension between following a false line and a true one. What I push them to is not play-acting: the limits of where their bodies can stretch physically, the truth of what sits on their face. At the first feeling of a lie, work is abandoned and started again. Some years after her rebellion, in the softness of middle age, you shaved your head, but only after a painting had been finished. The boys in one of the apple barns were marking each other with a set of electric shears in preparation for the grueling month of harvest – hair being one less thing to worry about; how their hands could not be distracted from the task of picking apples; that every second wasted sweeping damp hair from their forehead was an apple not picked, and two cents lost – and you had joined in. Your eyes were wild on your return; sunburnt face, arms and chest flecked with dirt from the shed. Your smile came from a place of successful initiation; of community membership renewed. The shyness that overtook you then, as you approached me, was the constant; proud yet still unsure. Everything else belonged to another man.

– You look like a convict.

– A laborer. One of many.

– Men, forty years of age, with shaved heads are those recovering from an illness. They're the only ones to go near clippers that brutal.

– I see it as more of a cure.

– You look odd.

– I thought you liked me to look odd. 'Not Everyman, but one particular man.' That's one of yours, isn't it?

– Now you're making fun of me.

– Only because I want to raise a smile from you. The sun's shining. I've drunk a beer and shot the breeze with some sound fellows. It's been a good day.

– And what a souvenir you have.

– It's ridden me of something unwanted. Don't you ever want to shed your skin when you've finished a painting? Start afresh?

– I start afresh every day. I've learned not to carry anything other than what I see.

– Even if you paint the same person. People.

– But it's not the same person. That's the point. You could paint the same tree every day for fifty years and it would be different each time. A similar object may be before you, but the speed of life alters it.

On this scale, Ben is a mere pilgrim, early down his path. Circumstances dictate that boredom floats under an ever-rising threshold. Irritations are swallowed; expletives thought but not spoken. He knows that he is the last. His next sitting will be with another painter in another studio. They will talk differently. If the artist is younger, Ben will be revered.

– I was thinking earlier of my grandmother, Anna. Granny Frances. My mother's side. When she was dying, the family was gathered from between the coasts. This was something like twenty years ago. We sat at her bedside for several days. Twelve of us, in all. Aunts and uncles. Cousins who were barely speaking to us because they already knew what was happening to Granny's estate and were angry about it. The tension was palpable.

– Who's dying? We're just painting here.

– Something happened after the first evening that dissipated all the bad feeling. Temporarily, at least. Granny had been fairly heavily sedated for the few days prior to our arrival, and the nurse had taken it upon herself to lessen the medication, surmising that clarity was more important than steam-rollering pain relief; those wards where sick people turn into morphine addicts near the end; folks prepared to sell their houses if it meant being injected with a shot that would knock them out cold.

– I've seen those people. I've had family that were those people.

– It was ugly before Granny woke up. That's the only way I can describe it. The sadness of everyone in the room, overtaken with ugliness. My mother, who I'd always thought as the most beautiful woman in the world; her face contorted with hatred as she prepared herself for the onslaught from her sister and her greedy children. My mother, who rarely confronted anyone, who shied away from arguments, turning into a gargoyle like the others, while Granny lay unconscious in her bed, sweating out the morphine. I'm not sure whether the nurse had this brainwave because of all the bad feeling, or from some misguided notion of a group of loved ones spending their elder's last moments in peace. A stroke of genius, either way, for when Granny came to, she surprised everyone by how strong and clear her voice was. 'I could feel your bitterness in my sleep,' she said, 'that's what roused me. I know that you're ready to murder one another over my decisions, but that is something you are

154

going to have to learn to live with. You have all this to look forward to: your years of arguing, piousness and regret. Everything that will both nourish you and make you miserable. But this can happen after I've gone. Until then, I want you to love one another, or at least, make me believe it.' Straight as an arrow, was Granny. Even when her insides were being eaten away.

– She had mettle.

– Selfishness, too. She wanted to control every element of how she went, including how we acted, what we thought. She was unable to stop what was happening inside her: cancer growing, strangling her vital organs one by one until only a shadow of life remained. But what she could do was to fashion our responses, to cohere the family.

– Safe passage.

– What?

– That's what my mother used to call it: those last days sat in the room of the dying, having reached that point where all other concerns become meaningless. 'Safe passage is all the dying want. Whether it comes from God or the garden, family or otherwise. They need reassurance that all will be well; that love is felt.'

– What about the old bastards filled with regrets? Those who die alone?

– Safe passage, still. They trawl their memory to find it from somewhere. If there's time.

– Granny had time. Two days, near enough. Her coherence wavered after that, slipping in and out of consciousness. Energy spent. The family was still ready to kill one another, but we made the best of it.

– Lay down your arms.

– We did, for a time. For Granny. Shared our stories of her, at her most tyrannical and her most loving. Songs were sung; those that came from the garden on the Fourth of

155

July and under the Christmas tree. Songs we thought we didn't believe in, but that she loved: 'O Holy Night', 'My Country 'Tis of Thee'. And in singing those, words mentioned from nowhere, picked up from the thread of another conversation and turned into a song, the room lifted. You know that moment in church when you're made to sing the choral, and somehow through the romance of the room – a giant cross bearing down upon you – and those manipulative chord changes, your chest suddenly becomes full; sound in voice and bursting with passion or belief? We found ourselves there: strength and love, good humor too, because everything else was put aside.

– And the day after that?

– We were back to committing murder. Shaking off the stink of death by threatening one another and hiring lawyers. The family was actually better behaved at Granny's bedside than they were at her funeral. They couldn't even sit together by then.

– Like I said, no one's dying. Your talk of funerals is premature. Sit still for a moment and let me look at you.

The man I see standing under the skylight is resolutely who is on the canvas. A build that is close to flesh and blood, bar the imperfections, the tiny, infinitesimal imperfections that make it so. The aim I must always strive for – unachievable, agonizingly so – is this: that life should breathe from layer upon layer of drying oils. The day that I can walk away from the painting without hating myself for it is still some time away. I will never be anything less than a harsh judge. It is the moment of weakness when I think otherwise; when traces of leniency flitter through the dust and fug as the late afternoon light fills the room; when my energy levels suddenly drop, making me light-headed and my hands numb and useless, severed for the good they are to me; the definitive point when I set down my things to signal the session has reached its nadir, and send you (or Ben or Vishni) away. It is the first moment alone after you have left, when the day's work is squared up; mistakes calculated for which I must atone into the night; a sound evaluation of any strengths. For as much as I am depressed by the failures I have marked onto the canvas – marks covered and re-covered with paint, but still there for me to find – the sight of Ben sitting on the floor in your fishing jumper makes me shiver with longing; wanting you to be here. For though Ben's features have been drawn since the first day, I have painted around and around several questions until they could no longer be avoided; those that can only be answered in the dark, ignoring all calls to join them in the kitchen. Would your pose adequately replace Ben's if you reappeared? Would the painting be junked if this was not so? Who is the painting for? When is the time to accept that such an appearance will not happen? When will it be finished? When will you return?

– I DON'T THINK that they were aware of the time difference. If they were, it meant nothing to them. They spoke as if they expected people from New York to be awake at all hours.

– I may have given that impression, for which I apologize.

– Was it vampires you spoke of? I noticed how they kept their distance once we arrived.

– They were shy. Unused to visitors in their home.

– And the filth. I was not prepared. The cleanliness of the country; the wholesomeness of the farms. How the air is meant to be pure; the vibrancy of the land itself. All the myths that had been peddled to me over the years were not created from those shacks. You were sleeping on the floor of a shack, John.

– This is how people live. The way things are. I saw no different as a kid, even on the Hudson.

– How that milk smelt. The dirt around it. I'm sure there's a reason for what you were doing but I don't profess to understand it.

You worry for Haley and Peg, and their place in a future America; how a life of living simply, of kindness, will be lost; something that you are unable to remedy or explain. They will exist for as long as the shacks stay standing and the cattle yield. After that, it is the kindness of others that they will have to rely on. The welcoming floor of other shacks.

Twenty hours in the town car has loosened St John to nervous chatter; skittish and babbling. There was assurance as he collected your things from the farmhouse and made a discreet contribution to your hosts for the trouble they had taken. What emanated was controlled softness, authoritative but empathetic, employed when dealing with clients who find themselves in reduced circumstances; patient, adaptable, but overwhelmingly in charge. Now the two of you are alone, he loses much of this professionalism, revealing the extent to which the journey has unraveled him. He despises himself for it but cannot help the speed of his mouth, the observations he feels he must share. It is payment in kind for his charity; for you to be made aware not only of the time spent to reach the farm and return to New York safely, but the very great expense in doing so.

– I consulted your doctors before I left. They did not advise a plane journey, so for that at least, we're in agreement. They would rather you were in a hospital, but then, they're probably saying that about Anna too, and we both know the outcome of that argument. Are you comfortable? Are you sure? As comfortable as you can be on the freeway. I wish I'd had the foresight to think about hiring a Winnebago or suchlike, but you're thinking on your feet when the phone wakes you at one a.m. Firstly, you settle your nerves, and are thankful that no one has passed. Secondly, you go with your gut responses: the car and driver you have on standby; adrenaline packing your bag and getting you out the door. I hope you have not found my attempts too shabby. It was the best I could think of in the time.

– You always look after me. I'm grateful. You can see it in my face, I hope.

– That makes me feel better. I won't lie and say that I wasn't worried – both for the condition I would find you in, and your pleasure or otherwise in being airlifted, so to speak.

– Fine on both counts.

– On one count, maybe. You've lost more weight. Your face is drawn. I thought they were feeding you.

– I ate like a king. When I had the appetite for it.

– I'm wondering whether we should find a hospital en route and have you checked out. Montana has a university city, so there will be an establishment there of some repute. Denver, failing that.

The dying know the hopelessness of their condition. There is nothing a hospital can tell you; no relief they can provide to stymie this. It is several hours wasted that could be spent elsewhere; gaining distance back to New York or another city where a further jewel may be held.

– Don't ask me about Washington. It's too far for a vehicle of this nature, even if we use the freeway. You look like you want to ask me. It's bursting from your face, like a man about to cough or sneeze, but I have to put my foot down.

– I'm not asking for anything. What you're doing is a kindness. I hope to be able to do the same for you one day.

– I'm sure that you will.

You are aware that his tone has returned to its previous state: the one he employed with Haley and Peg. He is on firmer ground now, confident in his role: benign parenting; the overseer. Sweat on his face drying from the car's air conditioning; his hand reaching to tighten the knot in his tie.

– I was wondering about your luggage. Was it given to your hoteliers, as some form of deposit?

– I don't have luggage. Never have.

– Your bag. It was on my mind as we helped you to the car, but an insensitive question to ask in their company. Certain sensitivities must be observed in the country.

160

– You mean, they would have blasted your tail off if you'd asked.

– As you're aware, I packed it tightly, so its absence does weigh heavily.

– I bought a painting in Kentucky. Something for her. A memory.

– With all of it?

– Most. Unsure of the ultimate destination of the rest. The mind can be an unreliable thing. Doesn't always tell you what you want to know.

Washington continues to weigh on your mind; the paintings found there which you will never see; the painting after Wendell drowned, more so. Wendell, in the forefront of your thoughts: impulsive and good-natured, inquisitive and wild as a cat. A twelve-year-old boy left in the care of you and his father for one afternoon, no different to afternoons you had spent before; a similar strength of benign parenting as you threaded flies, fished and drank beer. A competition between you as to who could net the biggest trout. Excitement burning in his eyes; certain that he could win. Turning your back for a couple of minutes as Edwin told dirty jokes, giving Wendell time to wade deeper into the water. You will not find a trace of the boy in Washington; only a picture that shows your disgust with yourself; disappointment in a body you had thought strong holding no sway against the current. How you were barely able to keep yourself from floating downstream, let alone reach Wendell, who drifted faster and faster. It is the hands you want to look at; those that finally stretched to their fullest and made contact with Wendell's forearm, tightening their grip and pulling him closer to you; regaining the equilibrium to balance him on your back and swim to shore. The hands are heroic. It is the face that makes you ashamed; the eyes that had been looking elsewhere. The

161

shaved head you were so stupidly proud of. This is what Washington holds.

You think of those who have spent their life reading books; novels that made the deepest impression that may have been read only once. Books intended to be read again, but neglected and forgotten. How to choose which books to reread when the reality of what is finite becomes clear? How to accept what must be abandoned? Your thoughts come to me and my needs; a question that you have asked many times before.

– Why do you have no interest in these paintings once you've completed them? They're finished and taken away, and you get to see them in a show for the last time, and then once more in a gallery or private house, if you're lucky. Does it feel like you've had something taken away? Or that you've removed something that you no longer need?

Of course, the answer is one that you're aware of, but still find hard to tally; throwing out its reasoning in the same way that I seemingly discard the paintings. What is kept, and what is held. It is never as simple as that, but as with the paintings themselves, what is seen is taken as truth.

You understand the need to make peace with a city you will never visit; that other paintings can now only exist as memory or on paper. Your glorified taxi has made that all too clear. The simplicity of your wish – riding train cars as you had as a teenager; crossing the country in any direction you liked, on whichever impulse, to see various paintings; the triumph of space over confinement; the freedom of thought – is now a futile one. Car, driver and self-appointed guardian now play a role. You remember the struggle of late childhood into adolescence; how hard you fought your parents for each scrap of independence. Now these shackles have returned.

The near darkness of the studio as you sat for the painting.

162

How the black of each corner matched the boy's eyes as he swam away from you. How they did not change even after you had pulled him close. Grabbing his arm and pulling him tight. Legs wrapped across your back; boots digging into your waist. How loudly you shouted at him to stay on. Still the eyes did not change. Your jumper afterwards, sodden and so dark. The torturer and salve that memory becomes in old age. All that you have left.

– I'M GOING TO ASK my assistant to come down for a couple of days. He'll be able to get on with things while we finish the painting.

– Whatever you think is best. We have the room.

– It's a better use of the time. Means I can sit in the studio and think of nothing else.

– I thought that was what you've been doing?

– We talked about possibly including this in the next show. We're up against it, time wise, if you are.

– You were the one who did the talking. Let's see how we finish.

– I'm putting myself at your disposal. Joshua arriving here will facilitate that.

– The telephone is being used less, I've noticed. That's probably been playing a part in your frustrations. The defeat of the modern age.

– There is only so much business I can conduct in my room. I need a man on the ground. A gopher in plain sight.

Ben is closing his deal with me. Future commerce reaches for him. His eyes and nose tell him that the finished painting is close; from the tension that sits on my neck and shoulders; that I am barely away from the studio, eating and sleeping there; the anger that comes so easily every time he breaks my concentration with another observation or story. He is a house guest who has outstayed his welcome; a nurse

164

disillusioned with the job. He complains frequently now, when his body seizes with cramp; asks for the skylight to be open more often, ostensibly for the oil fug to escape, but in reality because he cannot bear my odor: how finality clings so tightly to my frame. Twenty years ago he could sit and watch his grandmother pass because she was in a country whose distance was too vast to fathom; why he was able to sing with so much heart. Now it is uncomfortably close; its minutiae unwelcome; something that cannot be entertained.

Vishni is the one who accepts the burden of care; who bathes me from the couch in the corner of the studio; who quietly moves many of my things downstairs when she realizes how fast my mobility deteriorates. A chair of height and depth of surprising comfort, found and placed next to the canvas. The food, now simple and nourishing; soft and easy to digest: fish, soup, cooked fruit and strong, green vegetables. I do not eat all that is set before me, some days barely anything, my appetite taken elsewhere, leaving her to sit patiently with a bowl under my chin, one spoonful of broth at a time; encouragement, soft soap, matter-of-factness; whatever it takes for me to respond. Still I talk about the painting. Still she listens.

– I am sitting with a barracuda. He remembers that he has fangs.

– You have always been aware of that. He's family too.

– He will be worse when this boy arrives. Two scavengers ready to photograph and catalog. No item will be left private. Everything up for appraisal.

– Remember that he is your champion, and that we trust him. He will protect all this from being broken up. Stop the real scavengers.

– Where is he now?

– I've sent him to the store. Orla called to say that a parcel's arrived for you from Kentucky. Any idea what it is?

– None.

He needs the respite. Unprepared for what he sees, Ben now protects himself with his business; insulation from the reality of what is happening in the room. The first to talk over me when my breathing becomes labored; looking at a fixed point when I reach for the mask – five minutes of oxygen giving me the energy and clarity to continue. This is what the next sketch should be: myself with a brush and canvas and the oxygen tank. It fills me the way other paintings have done before; a new impulse attempting its dominance as an old one, the previous painting, dies out. Insurance of another kind. But I understand that this sketch will not come. It will remain in shadow, merely described.

I must finish the idea previously committed; one that I am no longer sure of; certain only of its physical presence in the room; its size and heft. Painting is not about impersonation, but here I have made it so. Tomorrow, I may feel differently, but today, what stands before me is fiction; the story of someone else. The man on the canvas is Ben; his arrogance and vulnerability in combat as posture and beauty compete for mastery. But the jumper he wears pulls my eye; that he is soaked through, his hair slicked. The softness of his face in contrast to the tension in his hands, gripping hard on the fishing nets at his feet. The definition of nerves, flesh and bone there; the fast coloring of his skin as he pulls.

There were days when I despised Vishni; each turn of her head and note in her voice aggravated me to near madness; angry with myself that I was so dependent on her frame for the paintings. Similarly, you; your compliance and surliness, each as reliable as the other; your openness, something that I was greedy for; needing to be repeatedly recorded. If you were here, this is how I would have painted you; not for any sentimentality over the jumper, but because mistakes can be corrected. The passing of time changes your point of view. Some things take longer to understand. Intelligence comes only from absence and atonement. How death is processed differently. You were against being painted; did not wish for death to sit so heavily in the room as it had done before. I disagreed. All I know. The body recognizes that this is a race against itself; the hand competing with the lungs; my breath fighting the speed of my thoughts. Ability over decay. Prosperity over rot.

Previously we battled nature. Only two years ago we went night swimming in the creek; our bulk pushing against mild currents and the detritus sent downstream following midsummer storms. We proved that nature could be over-come, fighting wild with wild, life with life, before we became frightened and allowed our bodies to turn in on themselves. If this is the last work, it must say something of this nature. I must be aware that it is so. It is a luxury to be in control of your end note; to know that the final coda is as you desire it. That I can finish the painting alone, happy in the silence of the room, reassured of Vishni's pres-ence nearby, and of yours, which never left. This is where we are. This is where I want to be found.

– THAT'S ENOUGH!

– I can't watch you like this. I have to do something.

– Stop pushing me toward the couch. I can't sit down. I want to lie here.

– Whatever feels best. If that's on the floor, so be it. At least let me take the rod from your hand.

– No. I need it. I can't explain.

– You don't have to.

– I'll give it back tomorrow. For now, I . . . I need something.

– Understood. Lie down now and rest. Try and close your eyes.

– I can feel you looking at me.

– That's not what I'm trying to do. I'll just be here in my chair, reading quietly.

You lie on your stomach, the sodden fishing jumper still clinging to your chest. Wendell's fishing rod stays in your arms, your hands cradling your head; fingers pushing hard against the floorboards, as if searching for a way to bury yourself. To let the darkness cover you as it has done Wendell.

I hurt so much for you that I want to abandon painting, knowing the pain in your face makes a mockery of everything we have done before. It's a false truth that can no longer be seen: a stack of canvases that should be left to

168

dry in the wind and flake away, layer by layer; a crumbling epoch that deserves to be forgotten. I am redundant but still capable, needing to record the face you have now, so that it can be the point from which you move past; for the pain you feel now to fade into memory. This is the only way that I can understand things, using order and method to make sense of chaos; knowing that I will remove the rod from your slackened hand as you sleep; the rug gently pulled away from your legs, exposing your bare ankles and the damp roll of your jeans. That your shoes will be kicked closer to the rug you lie on; a line that runs diagonally from your face to mine. That the mud from the riverbed drying in clumps around your heels will be as important as the streaks of dirt across your face.

How I will wait for as long as it takes for sleep to do its work. Sitting here, quietly. Waiting for the moment when you open your eyes, somewhere between unconsciousness and a remembrance of what has happened. The story your face will tell.

– Don't leave.

– You're fine here. You're safe. I'm still here, watching you. Relax your arms and try to sleep. Close your eyes. Let the sound of my voice carry you away.